KAT AND THE SECRETS OF THE NILE
by Emma Bradford

Kat and her aunt Jessie time travel back to nineteenth-century Egypt. Before long, they're members of a team that is unearthing the mysteries of a long-ago pharaoh.

There are other mysteries as well. Ancient treasures have been disappearing from the excavation site. Kat befriends Ahmed, son of the man who has been wrongly jailed for the thefts. Together they set out to find the real thief.

As they search for clues, Kat and Ahmed dodge dangers— from a fierce sandstorm to hungry crocodiles. But they soon learn that the greatest threat is a clever villain. And he's figured out that they're on his trail.

STARDUST CLASSICS SERIES

KAT

Kat the Time Explorer

Stranded in Victorian England, Kat tries to locate the inventor who can restore her time machine and send her home.

Kat and the Emperor's Gift

In the court of Kublai Khan, Kat comes to the aid of a Mongolian princess who's facing a fearful future.

Kat and the Secrets of the Nile

At an archaeological dig in Egypt of 1892, Kat uncovers a plot to steal historical treasures—and blame an innocent man.

LAUREL

Laurel the Woodfairy

Laurel sets off into the gloomy Great Forest to track a new friend—who may have stolen the woodfairies' most precious possession.

Laurel and the Lost Treasure

In the dangerous Deeps, Laurel and her friends join a secretive dwarf in a hunt for treasure.

Laurel Rescues the Pixies

Laurel tries to save her pixie friends from a forest fire that could destroy their entire village.

ALISSA

Alissa, Princess of Arcadia

A strange old wizard helps Alissa solve a mysterious riddle and save her kingdom.

Alissa and the Castle Ghost

The princess hunts a ghost as she tries to right a long-ago injustice.

Alissa and the Dungeons of Grimrock

Alissa must free her wizard friend, Balin, when he's captured by an evil sorcerer.

Design and Art Direction by Vernon Thornblad

This book may be purchased in bulk at discounted rates for sales promotions, premiums, fundraising, or educational purposes. For more information, write the Special Sales Department at the address below or call 1-888-809-0608.

Just Pretend, Inc.
Attn: Special Sales Department
One Sundial Avenue, Suite 201
Manchester, NH 03103

Visit us online at www.justpretend.com

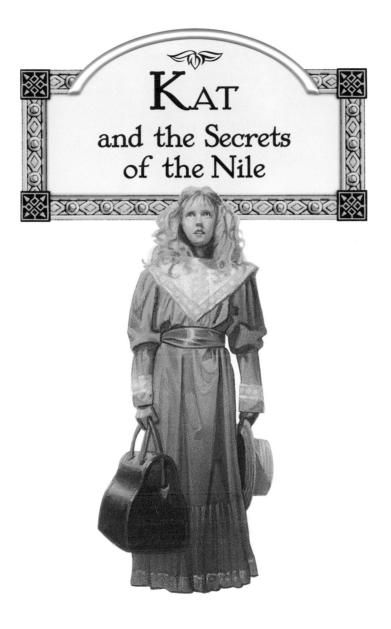

Kat
and the Secrets
of the Nile

by Emma Bradford

Illustrations by Kazuhiko Sano
Spot Illustrations by Tim Langenderfer

Stardust
CLASSICS

Just Pretend, Inc.
Attn: Publishing Division
One Sundial Avenue, Suite 201
Manchester, NH 03103

Stardust Classics is a registered trademark
of Just Pretend, Inc.

First Edition
Printed in Hong Kong
04 03 02 01 00 99   10 9 8 7 6 5 4 3 2

Publisher's Cataloging-in-Publication
(Provided by Quality Books, Inc.)
Bradford, Emma.
   Kat and the secrets of the Nile / by Emma Bradford; illustrations by
Kazuhiko Sano; spot illustrations by Tim Langenderfer. -- 1st ed.
   p. cm. -- (Stardust classics. Kat; #3)
   SUMMARY: Kat and Aunt Jessie time travel to nineteenth-century
Egypt, where they help to solve the mystery of the treasures that
have been disappearing from an archeological site.
   Preassigned LCCN: 98-65895
   ISBN: 1-889514-13-6 (hardcover)
   ISBN: 1-889514-14-4 (pbk.)

   1. Time travel--Juvenile fiction. 2. Egypt--Antiquities--Juvenile
fiction. 1. Sano, Kazuhiko, 1952- II. Langenderfer, Tim. III. Title.
IV. Series.

PZ7.B7228Kc 1998   [Fic]
                                    QBI98-681

Contents

CHAPTER ONE

A Timely Repair

L et me hold that steady for you," offered Kat. She gripped one end of the device on her aunt's worktable.

"Thanks," murmured Jessie without looking up. She was trying to put a spring back into a space that seemed too small to hold it. "Cross your fingers that this does the trick."

Kat couldn't actually cross her fingers, because her hands were busy. But in her mind she did so. Jessie just had to get the time machine fixed.

The machine still seemed magical to Kat. She found it hard to believe that it had already taken them on several trips into the past.

It was during their last trip that the machine had been knocked about a bit. So even though Kat had been eager for another adventure, Jessie had put it off. "Not until I'm sure the time machine is working properly," she'd said. "Remember, I'm responsible for your safety while your folks are gone."

While she watched Jessie work, Kat thought about her parents. They were far off in the Amazon, studying the plants of the rain forest for a year. Kat could have gone with them. However, she hadn't wanted to miss her first year of middle school. So her mother's sister, Jessie Adams, had invited Kat to stay with her. Kat had jumped at the chance.

Like Kat's mother and father, Jessie was a scientist who worked at the local university. Jessie was young, single, and full of life. She'd always seemed more like an older sister than an aunt to Kat.

On top of that, Jessie lived in a wonderful old house just across town. The house—and everything in it—had been left to Jessie by her great-uncle, Malcolm Adams. Malcolm had been known in town for his wacky ideas and even wackier inventions.

Jessie had discovered the time machine after her great-uncle's death. While sorting through his papers, she'd noticed an old notebook. It was filled with sketches Malcolm had made of his inventions, including a time machine. Then she'd found a half-finished model of the device.

Jessie had seen the machine as a challenge. For weeks she'd worked on it in her basement lab. Finally, with Kat's help, Jessie managed to complete the device. Yet once the machine was working, Jessie didn't understand quite *how* it worked.

Jessie's voice broke into Kat's thoughts. "Oh no!" she groaned. With a ping, the spring went flying into the air—and landed on Newton's furry coat.

Kat knelt next to her Irish setter, who was resting on the cool basement floor. The tiny spring hadn't disturbed him at all. Not much did disturb Newton—especially when he was napping.

Newton thumped his tail happily as Kat raked her fingers

though his fur. "Got it!" Kat announced. She stood up and handed the spring to her aunt.

"I have everything almost back together," sighed Jessie. "I just can't get this last piece to stay in place."

Kat leaned closer to study the problem. The spring went into a shallow drawer in the side of the time machine. Without the spring, the drawer wouldn't stay open. And that's how it had to be for the machine to work.

"Maybe I can do it," said Kat. "My fingers are pretty small."

She took the spring from Jessie. Squeezing to make it as tiny as possible, she eased the spring into place.

"It's in!" she cried.

Jessie tested the drawer. "And working."

"Great!" Kat exclaimed. "Now we can take another trip! You did promise, Jessie."

"I know," said Jessie with a smile. "We can leave once we have everything else ready to go."

"I'll get started," said Kat. She reached under the table and grabbed an old canvas bag. It went with them on every trip. "I'll check that everything we need is here."

She opened the bag and pulled out two medallions on chains. One was made out of silvery titanium, the other of gold. The medallions were what powered the time machine.

At the bottom of the bag was a book: *The Encyclopedia of History*. It had answered questions for Kat and Jessie on more than one trip into the past.

"It's all here," reported Kat. She placed things back in Malcolm's bag. She and Jessie had learned that nothing inside the bag changed during a trip. Anything else they brought along transformed to fit the period. Including—

"Money," Jessie said. "How about money?"

Kat patted her jeans. "I've got some in my pockets."

"I'll bet that's not all you have in there," commented Jessie. Kat had a habit of stuffing her pockets with odds and ends.

"Just the usual," said Kat. "My Swiss Army knife, a pen and pencil, and my notebook."

"All we need is extra clothing," said Jessie. "And we'll be ready to go."

"I'll get that while you set things up," offered Kat. She flew up the basement stairs, with Newton right behind. Much as he liked his naps, he wasn't about to be left behind when Kat was up to something.

They passed through the old-fashioned kitchen and into the hall. The shelves on either side of the hallway overflowed with Malcolm's collections. Model ships, old toys, science instruments, fossils. All that and more were tucked among the hundreds of books.

Kat hurried up the stairs to the second floor. She first stopped in Jessie's bedroom to gather clothing for her. Then she made her way to her own bedroom.

Kat couldn't have been happier with her room. It was so beautiful—and comfortable. A cushioned seat was built in to the space beneath a window that overlooked an old apple tree. In one corner of the room stood a lovely Japanese dressing screen. A statue of a famous Egyptian queen filled another corner. Bookshelves lined two walls, with a soft chair sitting nearby.

Kat grabbed an extra pair of jeans and a jacket from the clothes tree. Picking up her book bag, she charged back down to the basement.

She waved the book bag in the air as she re-entered the lab.

"We're all packed. Can we please go now?"

"Okay, okay, we're ready," Jessie laughed.

Kat bent down to give Newton a pat. "Take it easy, boy. We'll be back before you have a chance to miss us."

Kat wasn't kidding. They'd discovered that almost no time passed in the present while they were gone.

She scooped up her book bag, and Jessie hung the canvas bag over her own arm. Together they carried the time machine to a corner of the lab, near the basement window. Jessie slid open the small drawer at the side of the machine. "It's working perfectly now," she said with satisfaction. "So why don't you go ahead and put the medallions in, Kat?"

Kat placed the two medallions into the hollows at the bottom of the drawer. The silver one went on the right side, the gold on the left.

At once the machine began to hum loudly. Newton wagged his feathery tail and barked.

"Hold on," Jessie told Kat as sunlight poured through the basement window and hit the medallions.

The air around them turned misty and began to swirl in great clouds. In seconds Kat and Jessie were caught up in a whirlwind of motion. They closed their eyes, both wondering where—and when—they would end up.

CHAPTER TWO

A Last-Minute Invitation

When the whirling stopped, Kat opened her eyes. The mist had cleared. And as she'd expected, they were no longer standing in the basement.

As far as she could see, golden sand stretched out in all directions. Late afternoon sunshine—still very hot—beat down upon them. There wasn't another person in sight.

Kat took her hands from the time machine and glanced over at her aunt. Instead of jeans and a sweatshirt, Jessie was wearing a long gray skirt. A lacy white blouse, boots, and a straw hat completed the outfit. Hanging from Jessie's arm was a flowered traveling bag that appeared nothing like Malcolm's canvas one. As usual, the outside of the bag had changed to fit the time they were visiting.

Kat looked down and found herself in an outfit just as interesting. She wore a long skirt, blouse, and boots. Her book bag had become a leather knapsack.

And there was something on her head! Kat reached up and pulled off a hat much like Jessie's.

"This is neat!" exclaimed Kat. "Can you tell from our clothing what year it is?"

"I'd be the first to admit that I don't know much about fashion," said Jessie. "But I *do* know that women haven't dressed like this in nearly a century."

"Let's check things out," said Kat. She pointed to a hill in the distance. "We can head up there to see what's around. Other than sand and rocks, that is."

"First let's take the medallions out for safekeeping," said Jessie. She handed the gold medallion to Kat and took the other herself. Each tucked her medallion away.

Jessie folded up the time machine and put it in the traveling bag.

While Jessie was busy doing that, Kat looked inside her knapsack. "The clothes we had in here changed too. Now we each have a jacket," she announced.

Kat next emptied out her pockets. She found her pencil hadn't really changed—nor had her Swiss Army knife. But her notepad had become a tiny journal. And the ballpoint was an old-fashioned fountain pen.

By now Jessie had finished packing and was studying Kat's pile of things. "This all still seems more like magic than science!" She shook her head in wonder, then glanced around. "Well, let's find out where we are. Come on, pack rat."

Kat put everything back in her pockets and got to her feet. Together she and Jessie headed up the hill.

It quickly proved to be hard going. Small rocks slid underfoot, and the dry wind kicked up puffs of sand. The hot sun made Kat thankful she was wearing a hat.

At the top of the hill, Kat and Jessie paused to take in the view. "Look at that!" Kat whispered.

Below them the sun sparkled off a wide river that crawled through a broad valley. On the far side, train tracks wound into the distance. On their side, a cluster of windowless mud buildings hugged the bank. The town was bordered by fields of green and gold.

The scene was busy. People—tiny from this distance— filled the narrow streets. Boats of all types and sizes lined the riverbank.

"Okay," said Jessie. "I think I know where we are. We're in a desert. And there's a huge river." She studied her niece expectantly.

"Egypt?" asked Kat. "That's the first place I can think of."

Jessie nodded. "That's my guess too."

"Let's see if we're right," said Kat.

"Lead the way," replied Jessie.

Kat charged down the hill, with her aunt at her heels.

Before long they reached the outskirts of the town and slipped into the busy crowd. Veiled women hurried past with food baskets and water jugs. Children led donkeys through the dusty streets. Merchants, selling everything from rugs and candles to figs and bread, sat under palm-leaf roofs.

As Kat and Jessie neared the river, the activity increased. Kat pulled her aunt out of the stream of people to watch what was going on. A packed ferry was crossing the river, and other boats were tied up at the docks. A line of men and boys moved back and forth from these boats to the shore. They carried a variety of barrels, crates, and baskets.

"Come on," Kat said. "I want a better look."

They moved closer to the riverbank. Fine ladies stood on the deck of a tour boat. They wore lovely long gowns and shaded themselves with parasols. On the bank below, barefoot children jumped up and down, begging for coins. Meanwhile, gentlemen in handsome dark suits stood on the dock. Some shouted orders to robed workers.

For a moment, Kat and Jessie watched. Then Kat turned to her aunt. "I know how to find out exactly where we are and

what year it is," she said. She headed off toward a group of men who wore European clothing.

"Wait!" called Jessie. She grabbed Kat's arm. "You don't plan on simply asking them?" she said.

"Of course not!" replied Kat. "I'm just going to do a little detective work. See? That man is reading a newspaper. It's bound to have the date on it somewhere."

Kat wandered nearer to the group. As she passed the man with the newspaper, she pretended to trip.

"Careful, miss," said the man in English. He reached out an arm to steady Kat.

"Thank you, sir," said Kat. She smiled and curtsied. As she did so, she peeked at the headline. Still smiling, she walked off.

"We *are* in Egypt!" she whispered when she rejoined Jessie. "And it's 1892! We've gone back more than 100 years!"

Kat couldn't contain herself. She twirled in excitement—and bumped into a worker carrying a barrel.

"Many pardons," the man muttered.

"It was my fault," responded Kat.

As the man went on his way, Kat turned to Jessie. "That certainly wasn't English he spoke—or that I did. Was it…?"

"Arabic?" Jessie finished. "It must be."

"I wish I could figure out how the machine does that," Kat sighed. "I mean how it lets us understand other languages. It's sure a lot easier than studying a foreign language in school!"

"There's only one problem," said Jessie. "You won't remember a bit of Arabic when we get back to our own time."

By now she and Kat had passed the tour boat. Farther down the bank was a long flat-bottomed boat. A few workers were loading more crates and barrels aboard.

"Look at that barge," Jessie pointed out. "It's so full it barely floats!"

"I wonder what all those supplies are for?" said Kat. She and Jessie made their way to one of the workers. Speaking again in Arabic, Kat asked, "Where is this boat going?"

"To the place where we are digging, miss," answered the worker. "To the excavation site at Amarna."

Excavation site! Kat was so excited that she forgot to reply. But Jessie said, "Amarna? Well, thank you for your help."

At that, a tall bearded man who was passing by halted. "You speak Arabic," he said in a strong British accent. "And you are headed for Amarna? Thank goodness, you have arrived at last! And just in time!"

He snatched the traveling bag from Jessie's hand. "Let me carry this for you," the stranger said. Bag in hand, he marched toward the barge. Halfway up the ramp, he called back to them. "Please hurry!" he ordered. "We are about to leave!"

CHAPTER THREE

New Friends and Foes

or a second, Jessie stood frozen, staring after the man. Then she grabbed Kat's elbow and started forward. "Come on! We have to follow him! He's got the time machine!"

As they rushed up the ramp, several crew members began untying ropes. Others grabbed long poles to push the barge away from shore. In moments the sails filled with wind. The boat began to head up the Nile—with Kat and Jessie along for the ride.

"What's going on here?" muttered Jessie.

"I guess we're headed to the excavation," said Kat. She smiled at the thought.

"I gathered that," replied Jessie. "But why? Just who does that man think I am?" Suddenly she gave a cry of relief. "There's our bag!" She pointed to a rough wooden bench facing the deck railing. The traveling bag was tucked underneath.

Kat and Jessie made their way to the bench. Jessie checked inside the bag to make sure the time machine was safe. Then she sat down and took a deep breath.

"All right," Jessie said. "While we're alone, let's see what we've gotten ourselves into. I know you've studied ancient Egypt at school. So how much do you know about Amarna?"

"The name is familiar, but I don't remember much about it," admitted Kat as she sat next to her aunt. "I do know that a lot of Egyptologists dug around here. And I'm pretty sure there was a city at Amarna thousands of years ago. When we get a chance, I'll check Malcolm's book to see what I can find out."

Jessie, who'd been keeping a watchful eye on the deck, cleared her throat. "Perhaps we should discuss this later," she suggested softly.

Kat looked up to see the tall bearded man approaching again. "Excuse me," he said with a smile. "You must forgive me. In the rush, I never thought to introduce myself. My name is Thomas Benson. I am a member of the excavation team at Amarna."

Jessie and Kat exchanged a glance. This still didn't explain why they'd been hurried aboard.

Benson went on. "I was so glad to find you that I quite forgot my manners. Every time we have gone to Minya to get supplies, I have checked. I was beginning to fear that our translator would never arrive."

"Translator," echoed Jessie weakly. She paused.

Kat held her breath. Would Jessie tell Benson that he was mistaken?

But Jessie nodded. "I do speak Arabic," she stated calmly.

Jessie went on to introduce herself and Kat. Benson bowed to each in turn. Then he gazed at them thoughtfully. "I must admit, I am a bit surprised. I knew a woman was being sent. I just never expected an American." His eyes went from Jessie to Kat. "Or that you would bring a child with you."

13

"Katherine is my niece," said Jessie. "I'm caring for her while her parents are away. I couldn't have come without her."

"Perhaps I can help at the site," suggested Kat. "I also speak Arabic."

"Really?" said Benson. "I do not understand the language myself." Then he shook his head. "However, your help will not be needed, Katherine. In fact, I must ask you to stay out of the way. We have important work going on at the site."

Before Kat could reply, Benson continued. "I want you to meet another member of the team." He motioned toward a young man at the other end of the barge. "Mr. Howard Carter is one of our excavators."

As Benson moved off to get Carter, Kat spluttered. "Howard Carter! Why, he's—"

Jessie poked her niece. "Shhh!" she warned. "I know Howard Carter's the one who discovered King Tut's tomb. But that can't possibly happen for years. Look how young he is."

By the time the two men returned, Kat had managed to hide her excitement. She nodded politely as Benson made the introductions.

"Miss Jessie Adams and Miss Katherine Thompson, this is Howard Carter. Howard, Miss Adams is our long-awaited translator."

"Excellent!" exclaimed the young man. "We are truly in need of your services." He removed his hat and smiled at Jessie and Kat.

"The trip will take some time," remarked Benson. "May we join you ladies?" Without waiting for an answer, he sat beside Jessie. Carter took the empty place next to Kat.

Benson was soon deep in conversation with Jessie. It was a conversation that didn't seem to include anyone else. Kat felt relieved and thrilled when Carter began to speak to her. This man would make one of the most important finds of any Egyptian archaeologist. And here she was, talking to him at the beginning of his great career.

"Is this your first visit to Egypt, Katherine?" Carter asked.

Kat smiled. "Please call me Kat," she said. She went on, "Yes, it's my first trip. What about you? Have you been here long?"

"About six months," he answered.

"What do you do?" asked Kat.

"I started as a copyist," Carter explained. "Tracing the artwork found in the tombs. However, now I'm trying my hand at some digging."

"How exciting!" responded Kat. "Do you enjoy it?"

"Very much," said Carter. "But I am a bit nervous about working on one of Mr. Petrie's excavations. He is so well-known in the field. And he is most demanding. Things are done very carelessly at many excavation sites. Here we label and save even the smallest scraps of pottery."

"I'm sure you're doing a fine job," said Kat.

"I hope so," responded Carter.

They talked some more about his work and about sights along the Nile. Then Carter had to hurry off when someone else called to him.

Kat went back to listening in on Benson and Jessie's conversation. Benson was saying that their camp was several miles from the excavation site. Jessie would work in a tent at the site. That was where finds from the dig were brought. She would translate instructions to the workers who cleaned the pieces of pottery and statues.

As they rounded a bend, a movement near the bank

caught Kat's eye. "What was that?" she asked.

Benson shuddered slightly. "It's one of the many crocodiles found along the Nile. Best to steer clear of them, Katherine. The beasts have short tempers. And they can run quite fast if they have a mind to."

Kat looked at the swirling water. I don't ever intend to get any closer than this, she thought.

Before long they had reached their destination—several miles upriver and on the other side. As the boat neared the bank, Kat moved to the railing to watch. Crewmen shouted and threw heavy ropes to others on shore. In minutes the boat was tied up and the unloading began.

Kat and Jessie gathered up their bags and headed down the ramp. On the sandy bank before them waited a string of donkeys. The boat's cargo was being loaded onto the animals' backs.

As she stepped ashore, Kat heard a shout behind her. "You! Stop right there!" a rough voice barked in Arabic.

Kat turned back toward the boat. She soon spotted the speaker—a tall man near the railing. His brightly colored robe made him stand out in the crowd of white-robed workers. So did his angry face and quivering mustache.

The object of the man's anger was a small, dark-haired boy. Although the boy seemed terrified, he stared up at the man bravely.

"Little thief!" the man hissed. "Trying to make off with our supplies!"

Kat looked over at Jessie. However, her aunt was busy talking to Benson. In all the confusion, few people seemed to notice what was going on.

Kat hesitated. Should she step in? Then the man raised his fist. That did it. Kat charged back onto the deck. As she neared the two, she heard the boy say, "I am not a thief." He spread wide his arms to show that he had nothing hidden.

The man growled and began to reply. But Kat interrupted. "Wait a minute," she said, planting her hands on her hips. "You're frightening him. If you have proof he's a thief—fine. Just don't bully him."

The man seemed surprised to be addressed in his own language. And it was plain that he wasn't used to being given orders by a young girl. He glared at Kat for a moment. Finally he said, "This has nothing to do with you. He is a thief. And I know how to deal with thieves."

Kat stood her ground. "Do you have any proof that he's dishonest?" she asked.

The man gave a muttered response that Kat couldn't quite make out. What she did hear was her aunt's puzzled voice.

"Kat!" Jessie called. "What's going on?"

Kat swung around to see Jessie and Benson observing the deck. The dark-haired man also noticed. He grabbed the boy by the shoulder and shoved him aside.

"Off with you!" he snarled. "And do not dare stow away on one of our boats again. Next time you will not escape so easily."

The boy darted toward the ramp. As he passed Kat, he threw her a grateful look.

The man glared at Kat. In a low, cold voice, he spoke: "You might find it safer not to interfere in things you do not understand, miss."

CHAPTER FOUR

A Fright in the Dark

T he angry man marched down the steep ramp. He passed Jessie, who was on her way up.

"What was that all about?" Jessie asked.

For a moment, Kat and Jessie stared after the brightly robed man. They watched as he stopped to talk to Benson—in English now. Kat couldn't hear everything that was said. However, from the man's angry tone, it was obvious that he was complaining.

Kat shook her head. "I just tried to stop him from bullying someone. Maybe I should have stayed out of it. But when he looked like he was going to hit that boy…Well, I had to do something!"

Kat groaned as she saw Benson head their way, a frown on his face. "Now I'm probably going to hear about it," she said.

To her surprise, Benson ignored her. His words were for Jessie. "You must speak to your niece, Miss Adams. She has upset Omar, the overseer of our Egyptian workers."

Kat broke in. "It wasn't my aunt's fault, Mr. Benson. I'm the one who's responsible.

"Kat—" began Jessie.

Benson merely nodded to Kat. "Very well, Katherine. Part of your responsibility is to let Omar handle things in his own way. He is in charge of the workers. And he must make

19

sure that nothing is stolen. I suspect you have no idea of the problems we have with thieves."

Benson frowned again. "I trust that you understand."

In a soft voice, Kat replied, "I understand."

"Let us be on our way," Benson suggested. "The supplies are loaded, and we must reach camp before evening."

He led the way down the ramp.

Though Kat wasn't happy about being scolded, she soon forgot the unpleasantness. By the time they set off, she was caught up in the adventure of riding a donkey through the Egyptian desert.

Of course, it wasn't the most comfortable way to travel. The thin blanket Kat sat on didn't do much to cushion her from the animal's bony back. And every once in a while, the donkey just decided to stop. Kat learned to hold on tightly so she wouldn't shoot over the animal's head.

When she wasn't busy convincing her donkey to keep going, Kat studied the countryside. At first graceful palm trees swayed along the edge of the dusty road. Farther from the river, the trees gave way to rocks and sand. Soon Kat could see nothing ahead but hilly desert.

As the sun sank lower in the sky, the wind grew stronger. Now and again, a gust picked up the sand and swirled it over the riders.

It was late afternoon when the group arrived at the camp. By that time, Kat had had enough donkey riding. Every fold of her clothing was filled with sand. In spite of her hat, her hair was sandy as well. She was stiff and thankful to stretch.

While workers unloaded the donkeys, Benson talked to Jessie.

At last Jessie walked toward Kat. "I found out where we'll

be staying," she said.

Jessie led the way to a collection of mud-brick huts. The buildings were roofed with reeds tied in bunches and held down by rocks. Openings for windows had been cut into the walls. And the door coverings were woven reeds or lengths of cloth.

They stepped inside to study their new home. Two low cots jutted from one wall. A wooden crate served as a low table, with smaller boxes for seats. Other crates were stacked along the walls.

"I guess there are few frills when you work here," said Jessie. "Apparently some archaeologists bring servants along, but not Petrie. We have to do our own cooking and washing up. Mr. Benson is worried that we won't be able to stand roughing it. I couldn't tell him that we're used to a lot less on our camp-outs."

"No," laughed Kat. "Camping certainly wouldn't have been ladylike in 1892."

Kat opened a crate and looked inside. "There's clothing in here," she reported. "Some cotton robes—and this." She pulled out a long striped vest.

"That's lovely," said Jessie absentmindedly. She stood in the center of the hut, the traveling bag still in her hand.

Kat repacked the vest and moved on to other crates. "Plenty of dishes—and stuff to eat," she reported. "I didn't know they had canned food this long ago!"

"Is there room to hide the time machine in there?" asked Jessie, moving closer.

21

"I think so," replied Kat. "We'll just stick it underneath everything else. After I take Malcolm's book out," she added, reaching for the bag.

Kat hid the book under a blanket while Jessie buried the bag at the back of a crate. After that they busied themselves checking supplies, moving crates, and eating dinner.

By the time they finished their meal, darkness had fallen over the desert. So they changed into the long cotton robes that Kat had found in the crate. Then both crawled into their cots.

But they weren't ready to settle down for the night. Kat reached for Malcolm's encyclopedia. By candlelight she paged through the book. "Here's an entry for Amarna," she noted. "It says the city was built by the pharaoh Akhenaten during the fourteenth century B.C. He built it to honor his god, Aten."

"Does it say anything about Petrie in there?" asked Jessie. "If he's going to be my boss, I'm curious to know what he's like."

Kat flipped pages. "It only says he was a well-known archaeologist," she reported. She closed the book and slipped it under her pillow. "Howard Carter told me more than that. He thinks Petrie is wonderful. Even if he is fussy!"

Kat blew out the candle and stretched happily. "You know, fitting in here is easier than we imagined."

"So far," agreed Jessie. "Unless the real translator shows up," she said with a laugh. "Now that would be interesting!"

"Well, hopefully she's still a few days off," replied Kat. "Meanwhile, we have a chance to see what goes on at an excavation. Just think what we can learn!"

"It *is* an adventure," agreed Jessie. "But we'll be too tired to enjoy it if we don't get some sleep. We can talk more in the morning."

Kat pulled up her blanket. The desert night was surprisingly chilly. For a long time, she stared out the window at the starlit sky. In the background, she could hear Jessie's soft breathing.

"Egypt," she whispered to herself. "1892."

She fell asleep with a smile on her face.

~

The sound of voices woke Kat early the next morning. She jumped out of bed and hurried to the window.

Outside, several donkeys were already lined up and loaded with supplies. Petrie's men obviously liked to start work before the blazing sun began to beat down.

Kat moved to the other cot and shook Jessie. "It's morning. Time to get up."

Jessie slowly opened her eyes. For a moment, she looked around blankly. Then she sat up.

"Oh, Kat! I wondered if I'd dreamed what happened yesterday!" she exclaimed.

"Not a chance," said Kat. "Unless I'm having exactly the same dream!"

They dressed quickly. After a breakfast of biscuits and canned fruit, they headed outside.

Kat spotted Howard Carter among the workers. "Good morning, Mr. Carter," she called. "Here. Let me help you with this." She took an armload of supplies from him.

"Thank you, Kat," he smiled. "Are you ready to see the site?"

"I can't wait!" replied Kat.

"If you like, I can show you around," suggested Carter.

"We plan to excavate the whole city before we finish. For now I'm working in what was the pharaoh's Great Temple."

"I'd love to see it," said Kat. "What have you found so far?"

"Nothing important," said Carter. "First I must figure out exactly where the walls once were."

As they spoke, Kat noticed Benson talking to her aunt. He certainly acted helpful enough around Jessie. Maybe he thinks scolding me is helpful too, Kat thought.

But Benson smiled warmly when he spotted her. "Good morning, Katherine," he said. "I trust you slept well."

"Yes, thank you," she said politely.

"I was just telling Kat about our work," Carter said.

"Ah," Benson nodded. "And there's much to tell." He began explaining the history of Amarna.

Kat listened closely. She wanted to learn as much as she could about Akhenaten's city. Even if it was Benson who was teaching her.

Benson ended his speech when he saw that the workers had gathered. "Well, it appears we are ready," he noted.

At once they set off for the excavation site. The men walked. However, Benson and Carter insisted that the two ladies ride. So once again, Kat found herself bouncing along on a donkey's bony back. She wasn't sure she liked being treated like a nineteenth-century "lady." It seemed as if it would be much easier—or at least more comfortable—to walk.

As they neared Amarna, Kat peered about curiously. The site wasn't quite what she'd expected. All she could see were mounds of rock and sand. In a few places, she could make out tumbled-down walls of mud brick. It seemed hard to believe that a great city had once stood here.

"We're going down the King's Road now," explained Benson. He waved a hand to his left. "The palace once stood there." In the distance, Kat could see the Nile shining like a bright ribbon. When it was standing, the palace must have had a wonderful view of the river.

The group came to a halt. Benson led Jessie off to a large tent where she would be working. Halfway there he called back to Kat. "Remember, Katherine. Do not interfere with the work."

"I'll remember," said Kat, trying to keep her feelings from showing. Did he think she was a five-year-old?

She noticed an understanding smile on Carter's face. Kat grinned in return. She was glad that Benson wasn't the one who'd show her around.

Kat spent the next hour in the ruins of the Great Temple. Carter began by giving her a tour. Again Kat's first reaction was that there wasn't much to see. The temple had once been a huge building. Now little remained except traces of mud-brick walls and a few fallen columns.

Yet as Kat watched Carter work, she realized just how much was hidden here. The archaeologist combed through piles of sand and rock, explaining what he was doing. Each tiny piece of pottery he found was gently dug out and labeled. Reading about excavations hadn't prepared Kat for how hard the work was. Or how much patience it took.

Carter also told Kat about his hope of making a major discovery. He wanted others to share his excitement in learning how the ancient Egyptians had lived. Clearly his work was very important to him.

At last Kat thanked Carter and went off to explore the rest of the city. She was careful not to touch anything. And she stayed away from the roped-off areas where work was going on.

Once Kat spotted Omar's bright, braided robe. The overseer was standing with his hands folded across his chest. His eyes were on several workers who were removing dirt layer by layer.

I sure don't want to have another run-in with him, thought Kat. She headed off in the other direction.

By late afternoon, Kat had a fairly good idea of the site. The city had been long and narrow. At the moment, the excavation team was digging in the center section. This was where the remains of the gigantic Great Temple could be seen. Next to that, stretching out along both sides of the old road, lay the ruins of the pharaoh's palace. The team had already begun excavating that building.

The most interesting thing Kat saw on her tour was in the palace. Sections of the old floor had been uncovered. In places the colorful designs of the tile could still be seen. Now a roof was being built over the area to protect it.

Late in the afternoon, Kat settled down to rest. It wasn't long before Jessie stepped out of the tent where she'd been working.

Kat jumped up to greet her. "How did it go?" she asked her aunt.

"Fine," replied Jessie, wiping her brow. "And Carter was right about Petrie. He *is* fussy. Fortunately, I'm not expected to know anything about the stuff they dig up. I only have to know how to translate instructions into Arabic. And that I can do—though I certainly don't understand how!"

While they waited for the others, Kat told Jessie about her day. Then they started the long trip back to camp.

After dinner Kat and Jessie sat outside the hut for a time. When darkness fell, Jessie excused herself. "It has to be an early night for me," she said with a tired smile.

"I'll come in soon," promised Kat. "I just want to study the stars for a while longer. They're so much brighter here than at home."

Once Jessie had left, Kat decided to climb the hill that rose behind the huts. She wanted to get as close to the night sky as possible.

Halfway up the rocky hill, Kat stopped. She listened for a moment. Was there someone ahead of her?

Silence. Only the soft breath of the wind against the sand.

Kat started forward again. Such a beautiful night. So calm. So peaceful. So—

Too late Kat saw something directly in her path. She stumbled and fell face forward.

As she pitched into the sand, she heard a scrambling sound. It was followed by a low moan.

Who—or what—was out here with her?

CHAPTER FIVE

Uncovering a Plot

Kat's fingers brushed against soft cloth. It felt like the edge of a robe. There *was* someone here!

Slowly Kat rose to her feet. As she did so, she spotted a pair of dark eyes shining in the faint light. Then a figure stepped out of the shadow of the rocks.

"You're the boy from the boat!" Kat cried.

Though he hesitated, it was clear that the boy recognized Kat as well.

Suddenly Kat realized that she'd spoken in English. She began to repeat herself—this time in Arabic.

The boy broke in, speaking in his own language. "I can understand, miss. But I do not speak your language well." He continued, "Forgive me. I should not have been in your way."

"Never mind that," replied Kat, again in Arabic. "Why are you here? If Omar spots you, you're in trouble."

"I must stay here," he insisted.

"Why?" asked Kat again. "You're not working on the dig. And no matter what Omar says, I'm sure you're not a thief. So what are you doing?"

"It is a matter of family honor."

"I see," said Kat. She wasn't sure how else to respond. So she just asked another question. "Well, what's your name? Mine is Kat."

"I am called Ahmed," he said in turn.

As he spoke, Kat heard a soft rumbling sound. It took her a second to realize that it was Ahmed's stomach.

"Are you hungry?" she asked.

"I am not begging, miss," Ahmed stated proudly.

"I didn't say you were," protested Kat. She sat and began rooting through her many pockets. "Aha!" she said at last. "I thought I'd saved these."

She pulled out a handful of figs—only slightly sandy. "Sit down," she said. "You need to eat something."

Ahmed hesitated for only a heartbeat before sinking down next to Kat. He took the figs she offered and stuffed them in his mouth.

When he finished eating, Ahmed smiled shyly. "I am thankful for your kindness," he said. "And now I will be on my way."

"To where?" asked Kat. "It's plain you can't hang around here," she continued. "You can't live on leftover figs."

"I must stay here," repeated Ahmed. "To save my father."

"What?" asked Kat in surprise.

In the pale starlight, Ahmed studied Kat's face. Then he nodded and began to talk.

"My father is one of Mr. Petrie's stone cleaners. A trusted worker," Ahmed said with pride. "Or at least he was."

"What do you mean?" asked Kat.

"It is said that my father is a thief," said Ahmed bitterly. "That he stole the ancient things he cleaned and

A STONE CLEANER

sold them. I know that is a lie. I must prove that he did not. Until I do so, my father will not be a free man."

"Oh, Ahmed. I'm sorry," said Kat. This was serious news. Carter had told her that items were often stolen from excavations. Greedy collectors from other countries wanted the old pottery and art. They didn't care if what they bought was stolen. And from what she'd seen so far, many Egyptian workers were poor. It would be hard to pass up the chance to sell things.

"My father is honorable," Ahmed maintained. "And he is proud to work here. He says that Mr. Petrie does not simply search for golden treasures. He also finds and saves things that tell about the common people who lived long ago. He is more interested in our history than in the riches of past kings."

"So where is your father now?" asked Kat.

"He is being held in the jail at Minya," replied Ahmed.

"Do you know who said your father was a thief?" Kat asked. Though she thought she already knew the answer.

"Yes," answered Ahmed. "I was allowed to talk to my father once. He said it was the tall bearded man."

"Benson!" cried Kat in surprise. "I figured it was Omar who blamed your father."

Ahmed frowned. "In truth, you are right. Omar was the one who went to Benson. He said my father had something hidden in his sack."

Ahmed continued, "Benson opened the sack in which my father carried his lunch. And found pieces of pottery inside. But my father did not put them there. Someone else did!"

"Why, Ahmed?" asked Kat. "Why would someone do that?"

"I think it was done so Mr. Petrie's men would stop searching for a thief. Only the day before, an important cast had disappeared from the cleaning tent."

"A cast?" asked Kat. "What's that?"

"It is a copy made by molding plaster around something. And this cast was a perfect image of Akhenaten. It was made by putting the plaster on the dead pharaoh's face," explained Ahmed. "My father told me of it when it was first found. Mr. Petrie was most excited. Then the cast disappeared."

Kat nodded. "So the thief put some things in your father's sack. That way your father would be blamed for stealing the cast too."

"That is what I guess," agreed Ahmed. "Now I must find out who the real thief is. That is the only way I can save my father."

"Isn't there anyone who can help you?" Kat asked.

Ahmed shrugged. "My mother and little brother. Yet they know no more than I."

Kat climbed to her feet. "So there's only one thing to do," she said.

A fearful expression crossed Ahmed's face. "You are going to tell them that I am here?" he asked.

"Of course not," said Kat. "I'm going to help you clear your father's name!"

CHAPTER SIX

Problems Pile Up

The next morning, Kat got up early and dressed in the faint light of dawn. Before leaving the hut, she stuck some biscuits and a canteen into her knapsack. In moments she was climbing the hill behind the mud huts.

"Ahmed!" she whispered as she neared the top.

The boy's head popped up.

"Good morning," said Kat, sitting beside him. She plunked her pack down and took out the food and water.

"You really are going to help me?" asked Ahmed. He stared at her with wonder.

"I certainly am," replied Kat. "After we eat breakfast."

While she ate, Kat thought about the night before. Jessie had been awake when Kat came back to the hut. So Kat had told her Ahmed's story.

Jessie was quiet for a long time after Kat finished. Kat could almost hear the wheels turning in her aunt's head. Jessie liked to think things through—to consider everything carefully.

At last Jessie spoke. "This could be dangerous, Kat."

"I know," replied Kat. "And I'll have to be careful not to do anything that might change history." That was one thing they'd both agreed to avoid on all their trips.

"You're sure Ahmed's father is innocent?" asked Jessie.

"After all, Ahmed could be telling the truth as far as he understands it. He just may not know the whole truth."

"If you'd heard him, Jessie, you'd feel the same way that I do," declared Kat.

Jessie took her time before coming to a decision. "All right. Count me in. But only under one condition."

"And I can guess what that is," said Kat. "If things get dangerous, we go back to our own time immediately."

"Absolutely," said Jessie. "No matter how much we want to help."

After that Jessie suggested that she could keep her ears open while she was working. "I might hear something important. Meanwhile, you have to try to stay out of trouble."

Kat promised. And she really meant to keep that promise. As a result, she had a hard time getting to sleep. Ideas for how to help Ahmed kept running up against Jessie's warnings.

Now Kat wiped crumbs from her hands. "We need to poke around and see what we can learn," she announced.

"Today I will join the dirt carriers," Ahmed said. "That way I can be at the excavation site."

"That's exactly what I was thinking," agreed Kat. "We'll both do it." Kat had noticed girls as well as boys working at the site.

"I don't know," said Ahmed doubtfully. He studied Kat's shiny blond hair.

"I'm going to wear a disguise," Kat said. She reached into her knapsack again. First she pulled out the robe she'd used as a nightgown. Next came a long strip of cotton cloth.

Kat put the robe on over her clothing. Ahmed helped drape the cloth strip over the top of her head. He also showed her how to fasten it across her face like a veil.

33

"Well," he said, "you *almost* look like an Egyptian girl."

"Don't worry," Kat assured him. "I won't let anyone get really close to me."

She stood up, casting worried eyes on her knapsack. "Hmmm. I can't carry this with me while I'm pretending to be a worker," she said. "And I don't want to put it back in the hut. I'd rather my aunt didn't see me like this." She realized that visiting the site in disguise might not be Jessie's idea of staying out of trouble.

"Let's hide it at the bottom of the hill," Ahmed suggested. "I know a spot."

Once the knapsack was hidden away, Kat and Ahmed headed to the camp. They were just in time to join a group of workers leaving for the site.

"Won't you be missed?" whispered Ahmed.

"No," replied Kat. "Jessie knows I'm with you. And Benson won't care. In fact, I'm sure he'll be happy not to see 'Katherine' around today."

At the site, Kat and Ahmed tried to blend in. Large baskets were stacked near a tent. Ahmed explained that these were used to carry sand away from the digging. They each picked up a basket and set to work. No one—not even sharp-eyed Omar—seemed to notice the two new dirt carriers.

The work was hard, yet the workers seemed happy. One man stood to the side, clapping his hands and chanting. Ahmed explained that the man was a singer. His job was to keep everyone cheerful and moving along steadily.

The dirt carriers moved back and forth from the digging

to the sand dump. Kat found it tough to keep up. On the way to the dump, the basket weighed heavily upon her shoulders. And there was no escaping the heat and blinding sun.

On their third trip, Kat and Ahmed fell behind the others. By the time they'd emptied their baskets, they were alone.

"Okay," whispered Kat. "Let's explore."

They began to make their way from one part of the site to another. Sometimes they picked up baskets and joined the workers. Sometimes they acted like they were taking a break. With all the activity and noise, they weren't noticed. But they also didn't learn anything.

By midday Kat suggested that they find a quiet place to talk. Ahmed led her to a spot behind a great mound of rocks and sand.

They sat down, happy to rest for a while. Kat reached under her robe and began to empty her pockets. "I know I have bread in here somewhere," she said.

Ahmed watched in fascination as Kat's collection piled up. The shiny fountain pen. The Swiss Army knife. A handful of smooth stones. Her stubby pencil.

"Here it is!" said Kat. She pulled out some bread, wrapped in a cloth napkin. Kat offered half to Ahmed.

The boy accepted the food with a smile of thanks. "One day I hope you will share a meal with my family," he said.

"I'd like that," replied Kat.

After they finished eating, Kat started putting things back in her pockets. She was just about done when—

A noise came from the other side of the mound. Kat almost dropped the last item. She put a finger to her lips to signal silence. Then she got down on her hands and knees. Ahmed did the same. In single file, they crawled to the edge

35

of the rocky mound.

On the other side stood Thomas Benson. He was busily wrapping a cloth around something. A small shovel lay on the ground nearby.

Kat ducked before Benson could see her. She and Ahmed waited motionless until they heard the man walk away.

At last it was safe to move. "Benson! I knew I didn't trust that man," declared Kat.

"The bearded one is the thief?" questioned Ahmed. "Yet he blames my father?"

"I don't know for sure that he's the thief," Kat admitted. "I *do* know that no one's supposed to be digging here now. So why would he be snooping around and wrapping something up in a cloth? And what exactly is he hiding? Let's see what we can find out."

A search of the area showed nothing. "Whatever it was, he took it with him," commented Kat.

Ahmed's face fell. "It may have been the missing cast," he said. "But no one will believe us."

"I know," said Kat. "We have to find proof." She dusted off her hands. "We've got to keep looking."

The two headed back toward the palace. They spent the rest of the day there, working and watching. At one point, Kat was sure they'd been discovered. Omar walked by just as she was loading a basket with dirt. Even with her head down, she could feel the overseer's cold stare.

She was saved when someone called to him. Omar walked off in the other direction.

"Whew!" whispered Kat. "I may have been wrong about him being the thief. But I still wouldn't want him to spot us."

"No," agreed Ahmed. "My father has told me that Omar

is quick to find fault. Even with one he has not already labeled a robber!"

The sun was low in the sky by the time work ended for the day. Kat and Ahmed joined the workers on the trip back to camp. Kat's shoulders ached from lifting the baskets of dirt. And her mind was filled with worry. They hadn't discovered the missing treasure—or anything else that would help free Ahmed's father. She was beginning to wonder if they would.

Once they reached camp, many of the crew went off to spend the night with their families. In the confusion, Ahmed slipped up to his hiding place on the rocky hill.

Kat sneaked into her hut. A startled cry greeted her as she came through the door.

"Shhh!" she hissed to her aunt. "It's only me."

"Kat!" exclaimed Jessie. "Why on earth are you dressed like that?"

Kat explained as she removed the robe. Then she changed the subject from her day to her aunt's. "What about you? Did you hear anything that might help?"

Jessie shook her head. "Not much. Just some workers saying that nothing else has been stolen since Ahmed's father was caught."

Kat's thoughts went to Benson. What had the man been wrapping up? She almost told Jessie what she'd seen, but she decided to hold her tongue. It would probably take more proof to make Jessie believe that Benson was a thief. Kat would wait until she had something better to offer.

By the time they'd eaten and cleaned up, it was late. Kat started for the door. "I have to get my knapsack," she explained. "I left it outside."

"Watch your step," said Jessie. "It's dark out there."

Kat made her way to the hiding spot. Desert sounds surrounded her—the scurrying of small creatures, the swish of wings, the whisper of windblown sand. Last night the desert had seemed mysterious and wonderful. Tonight it was just a little spooky. She was glad to head back toward the huts.

Before she reached her own door, someone called her name. It took Kat a moment to recognize the voice.

"Mr. Carter?" she called back. A wave of Carter's hand helped her spot him. He was sitting near his hut at the outer edge of light from the campfires.

"I didn't see you at the site today," said Carter when Kat joined him.

Kat took a seat near the fire. "No. I was busy," she explained. "Did you find anything exciting?"

Carter paused before answering. "No, Kat. Just another long day. With nothing much to show for it." He seemed far less confident now than he had during the light of day. Kat was suddenly reminded of just how young he was.

"Well, maybe tomorrow will be different," she replied.

"I fear not," said Carter. "It is very discouraging. I have found nothing of real value. And, as you may have heard, one of the most important pieces Mr. Petrie uncovered here was stolen."

"That's hardly your fault," protested Kat.

"That is true. Still, there is one thing no one else realizes," Carter said slowly. "Mr. Petrie called me in to examine the cast. He knew I had some experience with such things. When we were done, he asked me to wrap it up. So I did, but…" The young man's voice trailed off.

Kat remained silent. So, after a few moments, Carter went on. "I put two more things in the same package. A clay tablet

39

with some interesting symbols that related to the sun god. And my sketch of those symbols."

"So those were stolen too," Kat said softly.

Carter nodded. "Yes. Mr. Petrie has said nothing of this to anyone else. Even so, I feel responsible for that additional loss. If only I had bundled things separately. Or at least kept the sketch in my notebook."

"It was just a mistake," Kat tried to comfort him.

"Just a mistake," repeated Carter with a sigh. "All in all, I think I have made a much larger mistake. My work here has been of no real value."

"I'm sure that's not true!" exclaimed Kat.

Carter shook his head. "I am afraid it is." He continued, "At least as an artist, I served a purpose. Others thought well of my drawings. So I have come to a decision. At the end of the week, I will tell Mr. Petrie that I am leaving. I can find another job in Cairo, copying ancient art. It is time to forget about digging up the past."

With that, he got to his feet. "Forgive me," he said. "I never meant to complain to you. Now I should let you get some sleep."

Head down, Carter walked into his hut. Kat stared after him. "Oh no!" she whispered. "He can't quit! That's not supposed to happen! If he quits, he'll never find King Tut's tomb!"

Now she had two worries. She had to find a thief. And she had to convince Howard Carter to keep digging!

40

CHAPTER SEVEN

Digging for the Truth

K at! Are you listening?"

At the sound of her name, Kat jumped. She'd been thinking about Howard Carter and how to get him to stay in Amarna. So she really hadn't been paying attention to what Ahmed was saying.

"There is nothing here to find," Ahmed repeated.

Kat was once again disguised as an Egyptian girl. Today she and Ahmed were searching a pile of rocks and sand near the ancient palace. They figured they'd find Benson's package in one of these mounds left by past diggers. After all, there weren't many hiding places in such bare country.

The mounds were called "rubbish" piles. That didn't mean they were garbage, however. Past diggers had only been interested in finding rare and unusual objects. They often threw out broken pieces of pottery and other everyday items.

Mr. Petrie wanted the old rubbish piles dug through too. To him even the smallest things were important because they showed how the Egyptians lived. So Kat and Ahmed had been very careful while searching.

Still, they hadn't found the missing cast—if that was what Benson had been wrapping up.

Kat put down the shovel she'd borrowed from the camp supplies. "There's nothing in this pile anyway," she admitted.

"But we have to keep looking. I'm sure Benson didn't have a package when he returned to camp last night. So it must be here somewhere."

"We do not know for sure that he is the thief," Ahmed pointed out.

"Well, he acted like someone with something to hide," Kat answered. "And that's our only clue. So let's find another spot to check."

"We cannot get much closer to the site," objected Ahmed. "Someone might spot us and wonder what we are doing here."

Kat knew Ahmed was right. She thought for a bit before saying, "I know another place we could try. Howard Carter showed me a rubbish pile near the temple. It hasn't been touched in years. And it's out of sight."

Kat set off, with Ahmed hurrying after her.

When they reached the mound, Kat checked to be sure no one was nearby. Then she began digging. She gently removed sand and rocks, just as she'd seen Carter do. She remembered to check every shovelful of dirt for pieces of pottery or artwork.

Ahmed dug too. Soon a small mound stood off to one side.

They'd been working for nearly half an hour when Ahmed sighed. "Are you sure this makes sense, Kat?" he asked. "Even if Mr. Benson is the thief, why would he dig up the cast simply to bury it elsewhere?"

Kat frowned. "Perhaps he was afraid his first hiding place wasn't safe," she suggested.

Ahmed sighed again. "I am not so sure," he murmured.

To herself, Kat had to admit that she wasn't either. Was she wasting their time? Was she wrong to suspect Benson? Maybe she just wanted him to be guilty. Maybe she was trying to prove there was a good reason to dislike him. Other than the fact that he'd scolded her.

All right, Kat decided. She'd give this pile another ten minutes. Then she'd call it quits. She'd just have to think of another way to find the thief.

Again Kat sank her shovel into the sandy mound. Two scoops later, she felt it hit something solid.

Ahmed heard her gasp.

"What is it? Have you found the package?" he asked excitedly.

"I don't think so," said Kat. "It's not cloth." Using only her fingers, she began gently brushing dirt aside. Slowly she eased her find out of the soft sand. Then she sat back so Ahmed could see.

"A statue!" he cried. "You have found a statue!"

"Well, not a whole one," replied Kat. She held up a piece of light-colored rock, finely carved. The long nose and wide mouth showed that it had once been part of a face.

"It is the great pharaoh, Akhenaten!" breathed Ahmed. "I am sure of it."

Kat lightly ran trembling fingers over the smooth surface. "Do you suppose this was part of a statue that stood in the palace?" she asked. She shook her head in wonder. "I can't believe I'm holding something that's over 3,000 years old."

"What will you do with it?" asked Ahmed.

That brought Kat up short. What would she do? How exciting it would be if she could show it to everyone. If she— Katherine Anne Thompson—could be known for her discovery.

But that could never happen. Katherine Anne Thompson hadn't even been born yet.

43

Kat's thoughts raced. Much as she'd like a reminder of her adventure, it wouldn't be right to keep the statue. Like the other treasures of the ancient city, it belonged in a museum. That way it could be seen and enjoyed by many people.

"I don't know," Kat finally admitted. "I guess I could just put it back. But then it might never be found—and it should be."

When Ahmed said nothing, Kat continued. "You could take it to Mr. Petrie," she suggested. "You know he pays well for finds. And your family could use the money."

Ahmed stared at Kat, his face serious. "Your heart is good," he said. "However, it would not be honorable for me to do so. This was not my find."

Now it was Kat's turn to stare. Ahmed's words made her ashamed that she'd ever thought of keeping the piece.

However, he had given her an idea. "Ahmed!" she exclaimed. "You may think I've lost my marbles. But what if I make it someone else's find?"

Ahmed looked at her blankly before responding. "Forgive me for not understanding. What are these 'marbles' you have lost?"

Kat laughed. "I'm sorry," she said. "It's an American expression. It means 'crazy.' Do you think it's a crazy idea?"

"I still do not understand," replied Ahmed. "So I cannot say if your marbles are lost."

Kat repeated much of her conversation with Carter. However, she didn't tell Ahmed about the tablet Carter had wrapped up with the cast. Carter had said no one else knew of it, so she didn't feel right about sharing that news.

Of course, Kat couldn't tell Ahmed about her real fear. That Carter would never discover King Tut's incredible tomb. She merely said, "I have a feeling he'll be an important archaeologist some day. If he doesn't give up."

"So how will you 'make' him find this statue?" Ahmed asked.

Kat sorted through some ideas before answering. "We'll use ourselves as bait!" she declared at last. When Ahmed seemed puzzled, she explained.

"We've been so careful not to be noticed. Well, what if Mr. Carter sees two diggers fooling around near the temple? Don't you think he'll investigate? And when he does, we'll have things all set up. We'll make sure he notices the statue. Once he's got an important find to his credit, he won't want to quit."

Ahmed nodded his agreement, and the two set to work. They buried the piece of statue again. Only the nose stuck out, pale against the golden brown sand.

As a finishing touch, Kat made shovel marks all around the area. She wanted Carter to see that someone had been busy there. That would make him curious. Hopefully, curious enough to check things out.

"There," she said. "The trap is set. Now let's bait it."

"What if he catches us in your trap?" asked Ahmed.

"That won't happen," Kat assured him. "He won't waste his time trying to chase two kids. He'll just want to be sure we didn't wreck anything."

Kat and Ahmed moved into place. A fallen column of granite hid them from sight. Before long they heard Carter giving directions.

"We don't want anyone else to follow us," whispered Kat. "So we'll wait until the workers pass by."

The two stayed behind the block of stone. Soon two workers came away from the temple area. Talking to one another, they headed in the opposite direction. A few minutes later, Carter appeared too.

"Okay!" hissed Kat. "Time to go!"

She and Ahmed threw the rocks they'd collected. The stones landed with dull thuds.

Carter turned in alarm. "Who's there?"

At that, Kat and Ahmed took off. They headed straight for the mound, their robes streaming behind them like white flags. Behind them they could hear Carter giving chase. "Stay away from there!" he called.

When they reached the mound, Kat bent down. She pretended to hide something. Surely that would catch Carter's attention.

"STOP!" shouted a voice. And it wasn't Carter's. Kat felt a rush of panic. She turned to see—

Benson! He must have been with Carter in the temple area. Now he was coming after them too. And his long legs had carried him right past Carter!

A horrible thought almost brought Kat to a halt. What if Benson stopped to investigate the rubbish pile? He might make the find!

Or worse yet, what if he caught Ahmed? He'd be sure to accuse the boy of being a thief. And he'd probably be believed.

Ahmed shouted, "Follow me!" He disappeared around the edge of a broken-down wall.

Kat followed quickly. As she rounded the corner, a hand reached out and grabbed her. In seconds she found herself in a dark hollow formed by rock and sand.

The two friends inched back as far as possible. They had barely slipped from view when running feet thundered around the corner. There the sound stopped.

Kat held her breath. She was sure Ahmed was doing the same.

"Dirty little beggars! Where have they run off to?" they heard. Kat realized with relief that it was Benson's voice. He hadn't stopped at the rubbish heap.

But had Carter? And if so, had he found the statue?

Kat settled down on the hard earth. It would be a while before they dared leave their hiding place—and before they knew if their plan had worked.

CHAPTER EIGHT

The Thief—Times Two

As the sun was setting, Kat and Ahmed crept from their hiding place. They fell in with the workers returning to camp.

Kat got back to the hut before Jessie. By the time her aunt arrived, Kat was again wearing her skirt and blouse. The robe—dirty and dusty—was stuffed under her cot.

"Kat!" cried Jessie when she entered. "Where were you? You missed all the excitement."

"What excitement?" asked Kat. She hoped Jessie wasn't talking about a mad search for two dirt carriers.

"Howard Carter made quite a find," reported Jessie. She removed her hat and sat on the other cot. "He uncovered some ancient statues in a rubbish heap that hadn't been touched in years. When I left, he had pieces from several different statues. And he was still digging!"

Jessie noticed the huge smile that spread across Kat's face. "It seems funny that he would have searched in that spot today," she added thoughtfully. "After all, he has so much work to do in the temple."

"Funny," agreed Kat, her smile growing even wider.

Jessie grinned back at her niece. "All right, Kat. That smile of yours says it's a lot funnier than I ever dreamed. What do you know about this?"

So while they fixed dinner, Kat told the real story behind Carter's discovery. Then she asked if Jessie had any news.

Jessie shook her head. "No. I didn't learn a thing that might help Ahmed's father."

"Neither did Ahmed and I," admitted Kat. "So we're going to try again tomorrow."

After eating, Kat headed for the center of the camp. Howard Carter had returned. He was describing his find to the other members of the team.

Kat stood nearby and watched. Carter was excitedly showing pieces from two statues. One was the bit of Akhenaten's face that Kat and Ahmed had found. The other seemed strangely familiar to Kat as well.

Suddenly Kat knew where she'd seen that face before. It was the same face as on the statue she saw every time she entered her bedroom in Jessie's house.

Kat moved closer to hear what Carter was saying. "And this is part of the face of Akhenaten's queen," he explained in hushed tones. "Nefertiti."

Kat noted the young man's expression. He'll never quit now, she thought. So that's one problem solved. If I could only manage to catch the thief…

Her thoughts were interrupted by the arrival of Benson. Kat watched him walk up to the group.

I'm still not sure about him, she thought. Had he been wrapping the missing cast in that cloth?

Suddenly she realized that she was staring right at a cloth-covered package. It was in Benson's hands! And Carter was making a surprising announcement. "I was not the only one who made a find," he said. "Mr. Benson did as well."

Kat watched as Benson unwrapped the package to reveal a piece of wall decoration. As everyone admired the object, Kat slipped away. So I was wrong about him after all, she thought. I guess I'll have to cross him off my list of suspects. A list that's much too short already.

With a sigh, Kat headed for the hut. She hoped that a good night's sleep might help her come up with a plan.

Yet Kat had no new ideas when she awoke the next morning. She lay on her cot, studying the reed roof overhead.

Sounds of activity outside made their way into the hut. Although dawn was an hour away, Carter and many workers were leaving for the site.

Kat rolled over. Jessie was still sound asleep. However, Kat made herself get up and dress. She decided not to go in disguise. Maybe I can learn more as myself, she thought. I haven't done too well as an Egyptian girl anyway.

Kat grabbed some food and slipped out of the hut. In the early morning darkness, she headed up the hill.

"Ahmed!" Kat called in a soft voice. A whispered response told her where to find him.

Kat handed her friend some of her breakfast. Between bites she told him about Carter's find—and about Benson's. Like Kat, Ahmed was disappointed to learn that they would have to look elsewhere for the thief.

Then they discussed their own plans for the day. Ahmed agreed that they might learn more if they split up for a while.

Kat rose. "All right. I'll find you at the excavation site later," she promised. Ahmed nodded.

Though the sky had lightened a bit, it was still hard to see.

As Kat made her way back to the hut, she heard voices. Someone was carrying on a whispered conversation in Arabic. The voices seemed to be coming from behind a nearby pile of rocks.

Kat didn't think much about it. It was probably some workers getting ready for the day. But then a few words brought her up short.

"I told you before. It is a risk keeping that piece here. Petrie is sure it was sold—and that the thief is now locked away. If it is found, the search for the thief will begin again."

"It will not be a problem," replied a second voice. "Today I go to Minya to get rid of most of the things. As we planned."

"*I* make the plans," snarled the other. He lowered his voice, and Kat couldn't make out what he said next.

Cautiously she moved closer and poked her head out from behind the rock. She could see the back of one dimly lit figure. Even in the faint light, the man's bright robe seemed familiar. It was Omar!

The other man was hidden in the shadows. As Kat leaned farther out, some stones moved beneath her foot.

"Shhh!" Omar hissed.

Kat froze. If they came around the rock, there would be no escape.

At that moment, a small creature darted across the sand. Kat waited fearfully.

"It is only a mouse," she heard the other man say. "Even so, we had better go. The sun will be up before long. Just remember what you are to do."

"I will remember," Omar grumbled. "See to it that you do so as well."

Kat heard footsteps moving away from her. Thank goodness! The thieves were leaving.

Kat waited for a few minutes to be sure she wouldn't be discovered. Then she set off to find Ahmed. She must tell him about Omar. And about the other man—whoever he was.

Kat was forced to admit that it couldn't have been Benson. If she'd had any doubts after last night, they were gone now. After all, Benson couldn't speak Arabic.

So who was the other thief? And how was she to find out?

By the time Kat reached Ahmed, she had the beginnings of an idea.

"Ahmed!" she called. The boy's head popped out of hiding.

"What is wrong?" he asked. "I thought you were on your way to the site."

"Our plans have changed," she said. She told him what she'd seen and heard.

"We are too late," groaned Ahmed. "If the thieves get rid of the cast, how can we prove that my father is not guilty?"

"There is a way," said Kat. "Omar said he was going to Minya."

"Yes. I understand that," said Ahmed. "But—" He stared into her eyes. "You are not thinking…?"

"Yes, I am," said Kat. "Maybe we can catch Omar trying to sell the cast. We'll just have to follow him to Minya!"

CHAPTER NINE

Danger in the Desert

ou are right!" Ahmed exclaimed. "We must start after him at once!

"Wait a minute," warned Kat. "We can't go up against Omar and his friend alone."

Ahmed stared off in the direction of Minya. "To clear my father's name, I would do so."

"You won't have to," insisted Kat. "My aunt hasn't left for the excavation site yet. We'll trail Omar while Jessie goes to get Howard Carter. They can join us in Minya, and Mr. Carter can take care of Omar."

"They could meet us at the marketplace," suggested Ahmed. "My family has a stall there."

"Come on," said Kat. "We have to talk to Jessie."

The two friends raced down the hillside. Kat led the way into the hut. After introducing Jessie and Ahmed, she briefly told their story.

When Kat finished, Jessie sat thoughtfully. "So Omar's the thief," she said at last. "You're absolutely sure that's who you heard, Kat?"

Kat nodded. "I saw him, Jessie! It was Omar. I don't know who the other man was, but we have to do something. If they have time to get rid of the evidence, Ahmed's father may never get out of jail!"

Though Ahmed said nothing, his eyes begged Jessie to believe. She smiled at the boy and said, "You're right. We have to find a way to stop Omar before he sells anything."

"Ahmed and I have an idea," replied Kat. She outlined their plan.

Jessie heard Kat out and then shook her head. "I don't know about this. I think I should be the one to follow Omar."

It was Kat's turn to shake her head. "I'm not sure that would work, Jessie. You need to get Mr. Carter. No one will be likely to believe me about Omar. Besides, as long as I stick with Ahmed, I should be safe. He knows his way around."

"All right," said Jessie. "I'll bring help as fast as I can. But I want you both to promise me something," she continued. "Be careful—very careful. Don't let Omar see you. And please don't do anything foolish."

"We promise," Kat responded. "Now hurry. We'll see you in Minya."

As Jessie set out for the dig, Kat and Ahmed headed for the donkeys that were tied up near the camp. They chose two of the sleepy-eyed creatures and climbed up. They didn't even take the time to put blankets across the animals' backs. That meant that the journey to the Nile was even more uncomfortable than usual.

At the river, Kat let Ahmed do some investigating. He soon returned. "One of the ferrymen remembers Omar," he reported. "He crossed the river on the last boat."

"Did he have anything with him?" asked Kat.

"The ferryman said that Omar carried a large sack," replied the boy.

A sack. The cast of Akhenaten had to be inside! There were probably other stolen treasures in there too.

"Let's go," Kat urged. "We can take the next ferry across."

Ahmed frowned. "It does not leave for two hours."

"We can't wait that long!" cried Kat. "We'll never pick up his trail if we do! There must be another way. Can't we take a small boat across?" she asked.

"We could," responded Ahmed. "If we had the money to rent one."

"I don't have any money," said Kat. "I gave mine to Jessie. Do you think we could trade something instead?" She searched her pockets. "What about this?" she asked, holding out the fountain pen.

For an answer, Ahmed grabbed the pen. He ran up to a man leaning against a small boat at the edge of the river. A heated conversation followed.

At last Ahmed motioned to Kat. "Come!" he called. "The boat is ours!"

They leapt into the boat, causing it to tip wildly. As the man untied the ropes, they pushed away from the bank.

"We should make good time," said Ahmed. "The river is with us." He handed Kat a paddle.

The strong current carried them swiftly downstream. Kat dipped her paddle in and out of the water, watching the steep banks slide by. No crocodiles today, she noted with thanks.

They had barely docked at Minya before Ahmed hopped ashore. He paused only to tie the boat in place. Then he was off, racing through the crowd toward the marketplace. Kat hurried along the dusty lane after him.

As they went deeper into town, the lane widened. Narrow stalls roofed with palm leaves lined both sides. From out of the stalls poured the odors of spices and the hot oil used for cooking. A rainbow of colors greeted them as well. Bright woven rugs, shiny brass pots, and braided robes were only a few of the items for sale.

Ahmed suddenly darted into a space filled with baskets of sweet-smelling rolls. Calling back over his shoulder, he announced, "This is our stall."

Ahmed introduced Kat to his mother and brother. Then he spent more valuable time explaining their plan.

At last Ahmed turned back to Kat. "We will talk to some of the other merchants," he said. "Perhaps one of them has seen Omar. He is not from Minya. As a stranger, he is sure to have been noticed."

Kat let Ahmed take the lead. He knew the marketplace and the men and women who sold their goods there.

Kat received some curious looks. However, Ahmed's questions were politely answered. They moved from stall to stall, past wooden cages full of birds and tables stacked with red clay bowls.

Luck was with them. When Ahmed described Omar for the fourth time, he was rewarded with a nod. "Yes," said an old man who sat behind a pot of steaming soup. "I know of whom you speak. He bought some of my fine soup today."

"Did he say where he was going?" asked Ahmed.

"No," answered the old man. "But he headed out of town. That way," he said, pointing.

The old man added, "I noticed because it was odd. He

seemed to have goods to sell. He even asked me if I knew of those interested in buying rare old things. Yet he headed into the desert." He shrugged at the strangeness of Omar's behavior.

"How long ago?" asked Ahmed.

The old man eyed him closely. "Why do you want to know, my son?"

"I cannot explain now, sir," answered Ahmed. "Except to tell you that it has to do with my father."

"Ah," said the old man. "I see. Well, he left only a few minutes ago. And he was on foot. You should have no trouble catching him. If that is what you think you must do."

"Thank you, sir," said Ahmed. He bowed to the old gentleman, and Kat did the same.

At once they raced off toward the edge of town. On the outskirts, they paused at a narrow path. It led through green and gold fields and into the empty desert.

Not quite empty, Kat realized. She spotted a colorful figure in the distance. The man appeared to be carrying a sack over one shoulder.

"That must be him," breathed Ahmed. "We have to follow!"

"Wait!" cried Kat. "We can't let him see us!"

Ahmed's shoulders sagged. Then he brightened. "Stay here," he ordered. He dashed back to the market.

Omar was still in sight when Ahmed returned. The boy carried two large baskets. A length of cloth peeked out of one.

Kat draped the cloth over her clothing. Next, following Ahmed's example, she lifted a basket to her shoulder. From a distance, it would hide her face completely.

They set out behind Omar. If he turned, he'd see only two farm workers walking by their fields.

But Omar never looked back. Kat and Ahmed watched as he disappeared around the base of a rocky hill. They doubled their speed, and soon they'd reached the rocks too. The sound of digging stopped them in their tracks.

Kat knew exactly what to do. Lately she'd gotten plenty of practice spying on people from behind rocks. She motioned to Ahmed, and the two silently climbed the hill. At the top, they lay flat and peered down.

Below them they saw Omar busy at work. With a small shovel, he was removing sand at a rapid pace. The large sack lay at his feet. Though one end was open, Kat couldn't make out the contents.

Omar finally stopped digging. He pulled an object from the hole and slipped it into the sack. Then he raised his head to wipe the sweat from his face. Kat and Ahmed were forced to duck.

They waited, listening. They heard Omar continue to move back and forth. He must be putting more stolen goods into the sack, thought Kat. There was one last grunt, followed by the soft sound of footsteps on the sand.

When they felt sure it was safe, Kat and Ahmed slid off the rocks. Once more Omar could be seen in the distance. He was heading back to Minya.

"He must have been hiding some things out here," said Ahmed. "They would be safer in this far-off spot than at the site."

"And now he's going to sell everything. What he brought from the site today and what he stole earlier," said Kat.

"We'd better hurry," she continued. "Jessie might be in Minya already. And she should have Howard Carter with her."

They picked up their baskets and set off. Kat wanted to

run, to get there ahead of Omar. But she knew they couldn't.

Before they'd gone very far, Kat heard Ahmed gasp.

"What's the matter?" she asked.

Ahmed pointed off to the right. Kat shaded her eyes to see more clearly. Just beyond a line of hills was what appeared to be a yellow fog. As the hills vanished, she realized the "fog" was moving toward them.

"A sandstorm!" cried Ahmed. "It will be here before we can reach Minya!"

Kat froze with fear. Now she could see huge clouds of sand, swelling and rippling. It seemed as if the whole desert was flying directly at them.

Ahmed grabbed Kat's hand and dragged her toward the rocks. But before they could reach shelter, the storm struck.

"Cover your face!" Ahmed shouted. "And put the basket over your head!" Kat barely heard him over the noise of the wind. He pushed her to the ground, and she immediately followed his directions.

The storm passed by in a matter of minutes. But it seemed to last forever. The wind whipped and tore at them in angry gusts. Where the sand touched their skin, it stung like the bites of insects. Even the baskets did little to protect them. The wind blasted right through the open weave, forcing grains of sand into their eyes and mouths.

As quickly as it had started, the storm died down. Kat lifted the basket and uncovered her face.

"Are you all right?" Ahmed asked in a worried voice.

"Yes," replied Kat. "Thanks to you. That was awful!"

"We were fortunate," said Ahmed. "It was only a small sandstorm."

They slowly got up, brushing sand from their hair and

clothing. Kat gazed around in wonder. The area close to them had been swept clean by the wind. However, the storm had missed Minya entirely. Grain still waved in the fields. The palm-leaf roofs of the marketplace seemed untouched. Everything looked exactly as it had before the storm.

Almost everything. For suddenly Kat noticed what was different about the scene.

"We've lost Omar!" she cried.

CHAPTER TEN

A Game of Kat and Mouse

We have to find him!" exclaimed Kat. "Come on!"

She and Ahmed raced back to the village. They didn't slow down until they reached the marketplace. There they split up to search for Omar. But when they met again, neither had seen him.

"He can't have just disappeared!" groaned Kat.

"Unless he is inside somewhere," suggested Ahmed.

Kat didn't even want to think about that possibility. "Come on," she said. "Let's walk through the marketplace one more time."

They were almost ready to give up when Kat saw a flash of bright color ahead. The same bright colors as in Omar's robe. "This way!" she shouted, speeding off.

Ahmed was close behind as she rounded a corner. And there—just ahead of them—was Omar!

"He doesn't have the sack!" groaned Ahmed.

"Well, he hasn't had time to sell everything," replied Kat. "We'll follow him and find out where he's hidden his sack. It must be somewhere nearby."

The two spent the next half hour playing a cat-and-mouse game. They followed as closely as they dared. Yet they didn't want to be spotted. So they did their spying from behind stalls and tall baskets.

From time to time, Omar stopped to talk to a merchant.

"I want to hear what he's saying," whispered Kat. She edged close enough to catch the tail end of the conversation.

"...many rare and beautiful objects," Omar finished.

"You ask too much. My customers have no interest in overpriced goods," muttered the merchant. He glanced nervously about.

Omar glared at the man. "Others will pay!" he barked. Then he stalked off.

"It sounds like he hasn't sold anything yet," said Kat to Ahmed.

They continued to track Omar as he wandered from stall to stall. The man's frown deepened after every stop.

Finally he paused to buy figs and bread. He settled down in a corner to eat his meal.

"It looks like he'll be here for a while," observed Kat. "We'd better hurry to your mother's stall. Jessie and Carter will be there by now."

"And then what?" asked Ahmed. "We do not know where he has hidden the stolen things."

"I have a plan," said Kat. As they walked, she explained. "We know Omar wants to get rid of everything. And that he's having trouble. So we'll make him an offer he can't resist."

"An offer?"

"Yes. We'll get word to him about a rich American visitor. One who wants to buy rare old objects. Someone who doesn't care what they cost."

"Who is this rich American?" asked Ahmed. "And how will we get word to Omar? He would never believe me. And I am sure he would not trust you either."

"Jessie will be the buyer," Kat declared. "I think Omar's

65

greedy enough to trust anyone with money to spend." She added, "Though I agree that getting word to him is a problem. If he knows ahead of time who the buyer is, he might get suspicious. Maybe I could disguise myself again."

"I have a better idea," said Ahmed. "My brother will go. Omar does not know him. And he will never suspect such a little one."

"Ahmed! Will your mother let him?"

"To save my father, she will. We have no choice," stated Ahmed. "Besides, I will follow him to be sure he is safe."

When they reached the stall, Ahmed's mother was waiting. She led them to the back of the stall and into her house.

Kat had barely stepped through the door before her aunt was at her side. "Kat!" Jessie cried in relief. "I was getting worried!"

Kat was just as happy to see Jessie. And Howard Carter, who nodded to Kat. Then her eyes fell on a third figure. Thomas Benson!

Kat pulled Jessie aside. "I asked you to bring Carter!" she whispered. "Why is Benson here?"

In the small room, even a whisper carried. Before the startled Jessie could reply, Benson stepped nearer.

"I think your niece feels I cannot be trusted," he said.

"Why, that's ridiculous!" protested Jessie.

Benson calmly held up his hand. "Please, Jessie. I understand. Katherine has been wise to suspect everyone. She could not have known what I was really doing at Amarna."

Kat's puzzled eyes went from one person to the next. "Okay, Mr. Benson," she said. "I'm listening."

"First let me show you something that may put your mind at ease." He reached into his coat and pulled out a leather case. He held it out so Kat could read the identification papers inside.

"'Inspector of Antiquities,'" Kat read.

"Yes," said Benson. "I am in charge of safeguarding the treasures found at the excavation. For that reason, I too have been trying to catch the thief. However, it seems that you've been more successful than I have."

In Arabic, Kat spoke quickly to Ahmed and his family. After she'd explained the situation to them, she turned back to Benson. Blushing, she stammered, "I...I'm sorry. I had no idea."

"That is quite all right," said Benson smoothly. "Just tell me where I can find Omar."

"And you'll see that Ahmed's father is cleared of all charges?" asked Kat.

Benson glanced at the family. "As soon as possible."

"We know where Omar is," said Kat. "And we have a plan for catching him. We'll do it when he tries to sell what he stole."

"That won't be necessary," said Benson. "Just lead me to him."

"I'm afraid that won't work," Kat replied. "He doesn't have the stolen things with him."

Benson frowned. "In that case, I fail to see how I can arrest him at all. Perhaps this should wait until we have more proof."

"We can get that proof!" cried Kat.

Before Benson could reply, Jessie broke in. "Let's listen to their plan, Thomas."

But after Kat and Ahmed explained, it was Jessie who objected. "It sounds risky," she said.

"Not with Mr. Carter and Mr. Benson here," Kat argued.

Benson spoke up. "I still think we must wait."

Just as Kat thought she was going to lose the argument, Carter added his voice. "Kat is right. We must not allow this chance to slip by. We should try her plan."

With that, Ahmed's little brother hurried off to talk to Omar. Ahmed trailed along, keeping the boy in view. Their mother went outside to the stall and kept a worried eye out for her sons.

Meanwhile, Kat and Jessie settled on stools in the small room. Benson and Carter went into hiding behind a curtain. There they would wait until they heard Jessie's signal. When she said "Let's agree upon a price," Benson and Carter were to step out.

They waited in silence. Jessie kept staring at the doorway. Kat's right foot beat a rat-a-tat-tat against the hard dirt floor.

They both jumped when Ahmed's brother reappeared. "He is here, miss," said the boy. He silently slipped outside to join his mother.

Omar entered, a large sack in his hand. At the sight of Jessie and Kat, he stopped cold. His eyes darted around the room fearfully.

Jessie leapt up before he could leave. "Why, Omar," she said, her voice filled with delight. "I had no idea that you were also a merchant! If I'd only known, I could have saved a trip!"

"Why, ah…" began Omar.

"I'd love something to remember our trip by," Jessie continued. "Something special. And it's such a relief to be dealing with you. I know you won't try to cheat me. Or sell me anything that is stolen."

Omar stroked his mustache. Greed replaced the fear in his eyes. Kat knew what he must be thinking. Foolish Americans.

So easily tricked. Well, Omar was in for a surprise.

The overseer sat down and opened his sack. Carefully he pulled out bits of pottery and pieces of statues. Jessie exclaimed over each one.

Finally Omar swept his hands over the collection. "This is every-thing that would interest you, miss."

Jessie frowned prettily. "They're all lovely, Omar," she said. "But surely you have more to show me. I know smart merchants like to keep their best items for last."

"This is everything," Omar repeated. He held up the empty sack to prove his point.

Everything! Yet there was no sign of the cast of Akhenaten's face! Without that proof, would Ahmed's father be allowed to go free?

CHAPTER ELEVEN

One Down, One to Go

Omar stood up impatiently. "So, if you are not interested…"

Jessie protested, "Wait! We *are* interested. Let's agree upon a price."

At her words, the curtain was swept aside. Benson charged out, with Carter right on his heels.

Omar jumped to his feet. "What is this?" he cried. "A trick?" He whirled and dashed for the door.

Moving quickly, Benson grabbed the overseer and pushed him against the wall.

Omar's eyes glittered. "I will—"

Benson interrupted. "Silence, thief!" he ordered. "Save your protests. You and I both know the truth in this matter."

Omar stared at Benson for a moment. At last his shoulders slumped, and he fell strangely quiet. He didn't speak even when Benson tied his hands behind him.

"Well done," said Carter to Jessie and Kat. "We owe you a great deal."

"Perhaps you will see the ladies safely back to camp," suggested Benson. "I can take care of our friend here."

As he spoke, he began to pack the stolen goods into the overseer's sack. "I'll bring these things along with me," he said.

"There's no need to do that, Thomas," responded Carter.

"You take care of Omar. I will make sure that these are returned to the site. Mr. Petrie will be disappointed that the cast wasn't recovered. However, he will want to see what *was* found." He took the heavy sack from Benson's hand.

"These items might be needed as evidence," said Benson.

Carter smiled. "Have no fear. I will keep track of everything." Then he asked, "Are you sure you do not wish me to go with you? Omar could be dangerous."

"Thank you, Howard. But I think I can manage alone," Benson replied. "The jail is just down the street."

At that, Kat spoke up. "What about Ahmed's father?" she asked hopefully.

Benson paused before answering. "I am very sorry, Katherine. As long as the cast is missing, the boy's father is still a suspect."

"But why?" cried Kat. "We know Omar was one of the thieves. And Ahmed's father can't be the other man I heard. He was locked up in jail the whole time."

Benson shook his head. "The jailers will demand more proof than that. There could be more than two men involved."

The tall Englishman looked at Omar. "Tell me the truth, you miserable soul," he demanded. "Is the boy's father part of your band of thieves?"

Omar just stared back blankly. After the question was repeated, he muttered, "He is."

Ahmed darted toward the overseer. "You lie!" he shouted. "My father is no thief!"

Carter gently grasped one of the boy's arms. "I am truly

sorry, Ahmed," he said. "Mr. Benson is right. Your father will have to stay in jail until we settle this matter. Meanwhile, I think you should come back to the camp with us. I want to hear more about how you and Kat learned of Omar's guilt."

"Thank you, Howard," Benson said. "Now I had best get this one taken care of." He herded Omar outside.

As the two men left, Ahmed rubbed a sleeve across his eyes. Kat knew he was fighting back tears.

The return trip to camp was a quiet one. Ahmed stood near the railing of the ferry, his eyes fixed on the water. Kat knew her friend was remembering his mother's sadness. She'd wept upon hearing the news that her husband was to remain in jail.

After what seemed like an endless trip by boat and donkey, they arrived at the camp. Carter and Ahmed went off to talk to Petrie. Jessie and Kat made their excuses and headed for their own hut.

"Oh, Jessie!" cried Kat, sinking onto her cot. "I was sure Omar would have the cast! But he didn't. So Ahmed's father is still in jail."

"Well, you tried," her aunt said softly. "Besides, we're not certain that Omar *did* take the cast."

"Remember what I overheard, though," said Kat. "I know that Omar had to be talking about the cast. It's the most important thing that's been stolen from the site. I just need to figure out what he did with it."

For a while, they both lay on their cots without speaking. At last Kat sat up. "This is hopeless. I have to get some fresh air."

"I'll come too," said Jessie, rising from her cot. They

walked outside.

Benson had returned and was heading to his hut. "Mr. Benson," shouted Kat as she ran toward him. "I have to talk to you."

The bearded man looked impatient. "Katherine, I know what you want to say. And I have already told you that Ahmed's father cannot be set free—yet."

He continued, "I understand that you want to help the boy. I do too. However, my job is to be sure that the treasures we find are protected. So nothing further can be done until all the thieves have been discovered. Hopefully, the missing cast and tablet will be recovered as well."

"But—" began Kat.

"That is all I have to say on the subject," interrupted Benson. He nodded politely to Jessie, who stood nearby. Then he pushed aside the door covering and entered his hut.

Once he was out of earshot, Kat tugged on her aunt's sleeve. "Jessie, did you hear what he said?"

"Yes. I'm afraid there's nothing more we can—"

"No, that's not what I meant!" Kat hurriedly broke in. "Benson just said something to me he couldn't possibly know. Something only Petrie and Howard Carter were aware of. He knows that there's also a tablet missing."

She went on to tell Jessie what Carter had said about the tablet he'd wrapped up with the plaster cast.

Jessie's look of confusion turned to one of understanding. "How could he know that? Unless…"

Kat finished for her. "Unless he's the other thief!"

CHAPTER TWELVE

The Trap Is Sprung

Jessie shook her head. "This doesn't make sense, Kat. Benson is an inspector. His job is to stop thieves."

"Those identification papers of his could be fake—or stolen," replied Kat. "And anyone can say they're something they're not. Look at us. We're not exactly who people think we are."

"We need more proof," commented Jessie. "We can't go to Carter or Petrie with what we have now."

"I know. And I've got an idea," declared Kat. "We'll trap Benson in one of his lies."

"Trap Benson?" echoed Jessie. "How?"

Kat explained her plan. When she finished, Jessie nodded. "It just might work," she said. "And I certainly can't come up with a better idea."

That evening members of the excavation team gathered around the campfire. There was a lot of talk about Omar and his thefts. Carter spoke of how much the team owed to Kat, Jessie, and Ahmed. Kat and Jessie smiled. Ahmed, however, didn't even raise his head.

"Thanks to you three," Carter declared, "many missing pieces have been recovered. Mr. Petrie is most pleased. I'm sure that he will be thanking you personally."

Benson spoke up. "Yes, we are all grateful for your help."

Jessie turned to Ahmed. Speaking in Arabic, she said, "Perhaps Mr. Petrie will want to hire you as a worker. Considering how helpful you've been."

Ahmed gazed at his folded hands and nodded quietly.

Jessie patted his shoulder. Then she smiled at Benson. "Our thanks also go to you, Thomas. We couldn't have caught Omar without you," she added, still speaking in Arabic.

Carter stared at Jessie, a puzzled expression on his face. But Benson just returned Jessie's smile. "It was my pleasure," he murmured.

At that, Kat leaned forward. "Why, Mr. Benson! What a surprise!" she cried. "You told us you didn't know a word of Arabic. Yet you appeared to understand quite well when Jessie spoke it to you just now!"

"What is going on?" asked Carter.

"It was a trick," Kat explained. "And Benson fell for it. He's been telling everybody he doesn't understand Arabic. That's why I didn't suspect him of being the other man I heard this morning. Now it seems that he's been lying. It makes me think that he *is* the other thief."

Benson began to sputter. "Katherine, you are letting your imagination run away with you. We are in Egypt, after all. There is hardly a shortage of people who speak Arabic."

"*Do* you know Arabic, Thomas?" asked Carter quietly.

"I know a bit now, Howard," replied Benson. He forced a smile. "I have been trying to learn. I simply have not wished to practice my skills in public." He fastened a cool glance on Kat. "After all, if a child can learn the language, surely I can."

Kat wasn't about to give up. "If you're not the other thief, I have a question," she said. "How did you know that something else was wrapped up with the missing cast?"

At her words, Carter gasped.

"I am sure someone mentioned it to me," Benson said. "After all, it is my responsibility to know everything about the treasures found here."

Benson rose to his feet. "I have had quite enough of this conversation. You have seen my identification papers. You know I am working for Mr. Petrie—to find the thieves."

He boldly swept his eyes over the circle of listeners. "I will also remind you that I recently handed over a valuable find to Howard. Hardly the work of a thief."

"Unless the thief wanted to look innocent," muttered Kat. But she sensed that at this point, Benson had won.

The Englishman turned to Jessie. "It seems your niece continues to suspect me," he said. "I certainly hope that you do not feel the same way."

Jessie smiled back at him. "Forgive me, Thomas. For a minute, I did wonder. Thank you for explaining things." She ignored Kat's deep frown. "Kat is just upset because Ahmed's father hasn't been freed."

"I understand," Benson said. "Now if you will excuse me..." Nodding to Jessie and Carter—and ignoring Kat—he headed to his hut.

"Mr. Carter?" began Kat in a soft, questioning voice.

"I am sorry, Kat," replied Carter. "I agree that Thomas said he did not speak Arabic. And I thought Mr. Petrie had not

THE TRAP IS SPRUNG

mentioned the other item I wrapped up with the cast. But I may be mistaken."

He continued, "Remember, Inspector of Antiquities is an important position. Mr. Petrie would have checked before asking Benson to join our team."

Carter stood up. "For now I suggest that we all get a good night's rest. It has been a most interesting day."

The young man bowed slightly and headed off. And, a short time later, Kat and Jessie bid good evening to Ahmed. The boy said he planned to return to Minya that night.

In the darkness, aunt and niece made their way to their hut. Once they were inside, Kat began pacing back and forth. "I'm sure Benson knows what's in that package because he's seen it!" she exclaimed.

"I agree," said Jessie in a calm voice. "Though I had a hard time believing it at first, I'm sure you're right. Something about his attitude tells me that Thomas Benson is the other thief."

Kat gave her aunt a surprised look. "But you were so nice to him a few minutes ago," she protested.

"That's right," Jessie agreed. "He's not the only one who can be two-faced. I saw we weren't going to win this round. So I decided to play along with him for now."

Kat sighed. "If I could just convince someone else."

"Let's sleep on it," said Jessie. "Tomorrow we'll see what the two of us can do."

~

The next morning, as Kat and Jessie ate breakfast, they discussed their plans.

"Until we have additional proof, we shouldn't say anything

more about suspecting Benson," warned Jessie.

"I know," agreed Kat. "We'll let him think he's got everyone fooled. But we'll keep searching for proof that he's the other thief."

Jessie went outside to see what was going on. Meanwhile, Kat wrapped up bread and cheese for their lunch.

Jessie was back in a matter of minutes. "Carter and most of the workers have gone to the site," she reported. "But it looks like Benson is getting a late start today. Just like us."

"Are you sure he's still here?" Kat asked.

"Well, I haven't actually seen him," said Jessie. "One of the workers told me Benson hadn't gone with the others."

"Funny. He usually leaves early," said Kat. She walked outside, with Jessie close behind her.

A stillness hung over the camp. Most of the huts were deserted. Their door coverings were drawn back to let the desert breezes blow through. But Benson's still hung in place.

Kat raced to Benson's doorway. "Mr. Benson," she called. "May I talk to you?"

There was no reply.

Kat turned to Jessie. "Well?" she said.

Jessie nodded. "Let's go in."

"Mr. Benson?" called Kat once more. When there was no answer, she slipped inside.

Benson's hut was even plainer than their own. A single cot stood along the far wall, stripped of its coverings. The crate table was bare except for a half-burned candle. Not a piece of clothing or luggage could be seen.

"He's gone!" exclaimed Kat.

"It certainly seems that way," agreed Jessie. "We'd better be sure though. I'll check in the crates to see if his luggage is there."

She found only a few cans of fruit and some dishes. "Nothing here except—"

A gasp from Kat halted Jessie's inspection. "Look at this!" cried Kat. She reached under the cot and pulled out a torn sheet of paper.

Jessie leaned over her niece's shoulder. "It's a sketch of a clay tablet," she said.

"And see here." Kat pointed to letters in one corner of the paper. "This is Howard Carter's signature!"

"So there's our proof," Jessie said. "Benson is the other thief. He must have the cast of Akhenaten and the tablet that was wrapped up with it."

"And he's run off with them," added Kat.

A shadow in the doorway startled them both. Kat breathed a sigh of relief when she saw it was only Ahmed.

Her relief turned to confusion. "Ahmed, I thought you left for Minya last night," she said. "Why are you—"

Ahmed didn't give her a chance to finish the question. "You were right, Kat," he said bitterly. "Benson is a thief!"

"We're sure of that too," said Kat. "But how did you find out?"

"I decided to stay here instead of going home," answered Ahmed. "I hoped to catch the real thief. The one who helped Omar. And this morning, I saw Benson come out of his hut with a package under his arm. He looked all around to see if anyone was watching. Then he took off."

"When?" Kat cried.

"Several hours ago," Ahmed responded.

Jessie groaned. "We'll never be able to find him now."

"Not so, Miss Jessie," Ahmed assured her. "I followed him. To a place near the river."

"Let's go after him!" Kat urged.

"Wait," said Ahmed. "There is something else. Benson met someone there."

"What?" questioned Kat. "You mean there's a third thief?"

"No, only two," Ahmed replied. "The man Benson met was Omar."

Crooks and Crocodiles

pparently Omar never even got close to the jail!"
Kat angrily declared. "Benson just hid him out
in the desert."

"We should have guessed," added Jessie. Then she
addressed Ahmed. "Can you lead us to the spot where you
saw Benson?"

It wasn't long before they were on their way. At the same
time, a worker was headed for the site with a note for Carter.
In it, Jessie explained what had happened and asked him to
return to camp with help. From there Ahmed would show
him to the spot where Jessie and Kat kept watch for the
thieves.

Along with the note, she sent Carter's sketch. That would
be proof enough of Benson's dishonesty.

Now, as they tracked the thief, they questioned Ahmed
further. "The package you saw," said Jessie. "Do you think it
was the missing cast?"

"I could not tell," replied Ahmed. "I was hoping Benson
would hide the package somewhere and leave. But when he
stopped, Omar appeared."

"What did they say?" asked Kat.

"I did not dare get too close, so I could not hear everything. But I heard Omar say he would return at sunset. He

went off into the desert. And that is when Benson put the package into the water."

"Into the water!" gasped Jessie. "You mean he threw it into the river?"

"No," replied Ahmed. "First he put the package in the basket of a shadoof. Then he cut the rope and left it hanging loose. He stuck the basket, with the package inside, under the water at the edge of the river."

"A shadoof!" Kat repeated. She remembered Carter pointing one out on her first boat ride to camp. The devices were seen all along the banks of the Nile. Each consisted of a watertight basket that hung from the end of a long pole. When the pole was lowered into the river, the basket filled with water. Then it was raised and poured into a ditch. From there the water flowed to the fields that lined the bank.

"He must have used oilcloth to wrap the package," murmured Jessie. "That would be waterproof. He'd know a plaster cast wouldn't last long if it got wet."

"That was my thought as well," replied Ahmed. "Even so, I would have taken the package from him at once, before it got wet. But I knew I needed help."

Suddenly the boy halted. "We are almost to the spot," he whispered. Moving cautiously, he made his way past a rocky hill. Jessie and Kat followed.

Ahead of them, the river curved slightly. A broad, flat area opened up along the rocky bank. Resting on the sand was a small boat.

"They must be planning to cross the river in that," observed Kat.

Beyond the boat, the bank rose steeply. At the top, fields of grain stretched out into the distance. A shadoof stood at the edge of the river, its cut rope dangling above the water.

There was no sign of either Benson or Omar. Nor was there anywhere the two men could be hiding. Still, Ahmed ordered, "Wait here. I will make sure there is no one about. Then I will take care of the boat so they cannot use it to escape."

He slipped soundlessly along the bank. Once he reached the boat, he pushed it into the water. As it began to float downstream, Ahmed signaled Kat and Jessie to come forward.

"We have to get the cast before we do anything else," said Jessie as they joined him.

"I will make sure you are safe while you do so," offered Ahmed.

"I don't think we need to worry about Omar and Benson right now," Kat assured him.

"I do not mean the thieves." Ahmed motioned toward the river. "Look!"

Kat and Jessie studied the water. In the middle of the river, the current sped along in a swift, straight path. Closer to the banks, it swirled in muddy curves around several logs.

"I don't see anything," noted Kat. "Just water and logs."

"Those logs are crocodiles," said Ahmed.

Kat and Jessie peered closer. Now they saw a pair of eyes and a sharp nose at the end of each log! As they watched, a long, scaly tail rose into the air.

Jessie gulped. "We have to get that package," she said.

"What can we do?"

"It is said they will not attack unless they are hungry—or angry," replied Ahmed.

"And how do we find that out?" asked Kat. "Do we ask them if they've had a good breakfast and a great day?"

Ahmed picked up a handful of stones. "If they come near, I will frighten them away," he said. "You and Miss Jessie get the package. And hurry."

Kat and Jessie needed no other warning. While Ahmed moved nearer to the crocodiles, they rushed to the rock. From the water, several crocodiles followed their progress.

Jessie leaned out from the bank and tugged at the rope. "I can't pull the basket up!" she cried. "It's stuck in the mud!"

Kat climbed onto the rock. "Let me try," she suggested. "Hang on to me," she said as she got down on her stomach.

Bracing herself, Jessie tightly held one of Kat's hands. Inch by inch, Kat slid nearer the water. She kept her eyes on the rope—not daring to watch what the crocodiles were doing. Her only comfort was the warm grasp of Jessie's hand.

Kat reached into the water. She could see an oilcloth-wrapped package now. She also noted that it was tied tightly to the basket.

Kat tugged on the rope. But even from this close, she couldn't budge the basket.

She sat up and let go of Jessie's hand. "I'm going to have to cut the package loose," she said. "Otherwise, we're never going to get it out."

She reached into her pocket, pulled out her knife, and flipped the blade open. Then she lay back down.

"Hold my feet!" she called to Jessie.

"Kat—" began Jessie.

"I need both hands," said Kat.

Jessie couldn't argue with that. So with Jessie gripping her by the ankles, Kat slid over the edge of the rock. Sticking her hands underwater, she began to cut through the thick twine that held the package in the basket.

"Hurry!" called Ahmed. "One of the crocodiles is starting this way."

Kat felt her heart skip a beat. She sawed away like a mad violinist. The last strand split apart and Kat snatched the slippery package. "Pull!" she shouted.

Jessie yanked so hard that Kat flopped back on the rock like a landed fish. "Are you okay?" Jessie asked.

Kat caught her breath. "I'm fine. I'm just not sure that the package is."

She and Jessie scrambled down from the rock and up the bank. They wanted to put some distance between themselves and the crocodiles.

Ahmed watched as they opened the package, his eyes filled with unspoken hope. Slowly Jessie unwrapped the oilcloth.

"The outside is soaked. But once you get past the first layer, it seems okay," she commented. As she unfolded the last bit of cloth, the pharaoh's face gazed back at them.

"That's it!" breathed Kat. "The missing cast."

"The tablet is here too," said Jessie. She pulled out a piece of stone marked with symbols.

"It's exactly like Howard Carter's sketch," agreed Kat.

"Now that we have found the cast, I should return to camp," said Ahmed. "Mr. Carter may be waiting."

"Be careful," warned Jessie.

"I will," Ahmed assured her. "You must be careful too. The thieves could show up before I return."

Kat promised to keep an eye out for Benson and Omar. With a wave of his hand, Ahmed set off.

"While we're waiting, let's find somewhere safe to put the package," said Jessie.

"Okay," said Kat. "But I think we should make it look like it's still in the water. Just in case Benson or Omar happen along to check. We wouldn't want them getting suspicious before Carter gets here."

"That's a good idea," agreed Jessie. She removed one piece of oilcloth from around the package and handed it to Kat.

Jessie found a hiding spot along the bank and placed the package there. Meanwhile, Kat wrapped oilcloth around a large stone, then climbed back onto the rock. Leaning over the edge, she dropped the bundle into the basket. Jessie stood by with a pile of stones, ready to warn off the crocodiles.

Kat had finished and was about to get up when a voice sounded behind her.

"Well, well, what have we here? Looking for something, ladies?"

Kat and Jessie spun around. Not far away, Benson stood at the edge of the river. A smile split his bearded face.

"Thomas," said Jessie quietly. Her eyes went to the nearby pile of stones.

"Please, Jessie. Throwing a rock really would not be wise," he warned. "Your niece could get hurt."

With a helpless glance at Kat, Jessie let her hands hang loosely at her sides.

"You would never have thrown anything at me anyway, would you?" Benson asked smoothly. "You are much too lady-like for that."

As the man stepped closer, Kat jumped off the rock. The

moment her feet hit the bank, he snarled at her. "Not another step. I would be more than happy to toss you in the river."

Kat froze. The glitter in Benson's eyes told her that he meant what he said.

"Why did you do it, Thomas?" Jessie asked sadly.

"Why do you think? For the money, of course. There are greedy fools who will pay almost any price for the things we took. And I have a special buyer who is interested in the cast. Fortunately I held on to that."

"I still don't understand something," Jessie said. "How did you get Petrie to hire you?"

All at once, Kat realized what Jessie was trying to do. She was hoping to keep Benson occupied until Ahmed got back with help.

And it seemed to be working. Benson was happy to talk about his clever plan. He explained how he'd switched identification with the Inspector of Antiquities. "So I ended up with Petrie," he bragged. "Meanwhile, the real inspector is spending a little time in a prison cell in Cairo. Trying to prove he is not me," he laughed.

"I see," Jessie nodded thoughtfully. "And how did you arrange to have Ahmed's father blamed for the thefts?"

That was when the light dawned for Benson. "Jessie! Would you be trying to sidetrack me by any chance?" he asked. "Really, that is quite useless. You surely cannot expect a rescue party to come wandering by out here. In any case, I am a busy man. So let us end this—now." He started toward them.

We'd better think of something fast, Kat realized. The dangerous glitter was back in Benson's eyes.

Suddenly Kat remembered her first trip from Minya to Amarna. She thought about Benson's shudder at the sight of crocodiles along the river. That's it, she realized.

She let loose a terrified scream. "The crocodiles!" she yelled, pointing behind Benson. "They're heading this way."

"You really think to fool me like that?" laughed Benson.

"She's not lying, Thomas!" cried Jessie. "That's why I had these stones. In case I had to scare the crocodiles away."

She moved farther up the bank, at the same time calling to her niece. "Come on, Kat. Get away from the water."

Benson's face took on an uncertain look. His glance went to Kat, whose terrified eyes were fastened on something behind him. "They're coming up the bank!" she shouted.

The trick worked. Benson half turned to check over his shoulder. So he didn't notice as Jessie grabbed a stone. She threw it as hard as she could into the water behind the thief.

The noise frightened a crocodile who'd been quietly sunning himself nearby. With a snap of his great jaws, the beast swam off toward the middle of the river.

Benson noticed only the crocodile's sharp teeth—not the direction it was headed. At once he began to scramble up the bank. In his haste, his feet slipped in the mud and he fell on his face.

In a second, Kat had planted herself right on his back. Jessie immediately joined her. Their weight, combined with the sticky mud, pinned Benson in place. After trying to get to his feet and failing, he ended up begging. "Please let me go," he said, spitting out mud with his words. "The crocodiles—"

"They're long gone," said Kat.

"And you will be too," added Jessie coolly. "As soon as Carter and some men from the site show up. You see, we *are* expecting a rescue party."

Benson mumbled again, but they ignored him. "Do you have the twine you cut off the package?" Jessie asked Kat. "I think we should tie this thief up."

They soon had Benson bound hand and foot. Afterward they settled themselves nearby on the riverbank. Benson lay without moving, his eyes on the crocodiles that swam just offshore.

It was late morning when Ahmed arrived with Carter and four men from the site. Carter was overjoyed to find that they'd captured the thief. And he was nearly speechless when he opened the oilcloth package.

"The cast," he said with satisfaction. "How can I ever thank you two ladies?" he asked, gazing from Kat to Jessie.

Then Carter demanded to know where Omar could be found. At first Benson refused to answer. Carter's warning about the punishment for helping Omar escape changed his mind.

Three of the men went off to find the cave that Benson described. Carter warned them that Omar might be danger-ous. However, they all knew that the overseer was probably sleeping through the heat of the day.

The group was back in short order—with Omar and some more stolen pieces. It was clear that the thieves had been busy at other sites as well.

With both thieves in tow, Carter turned to Kat and Jessie. "Now, ladies, I think it is time I took these gentlemen to Minya. If you do not mind making your own way back to camp?"

Kat and Jessie assured him that was fine.

"I expect Ahmed will want to come along with us," Carter noted.

Ahmed looked at Kat, his eyes shining. "Mr. Carter has promised to see to it himself that my father is freed today," he announced.

"Oh, Ahmed, thank goodness," said Kat.

The boy threw his arms around her. "You are a true friend," he said. "You will always be honored in our house. Thank you, Kat. And Miss Jessie."

He bowed to them. Then he, Carter, and the rest of the group set off for Minya.

"Well, that seems to take care of that," noted Jessie. "What do you think?"

Kat watched as her friends disappeared over the hilly bank. "I'm ready," she replied. "Let's head for home."

CHAPTER FOURTEEN

A Queen's Smile

Before leaving, there were a few loose ends to tie up. So Kat and Jessie returned to camp to do just that.

Quickly they packed their belongings. That left only one task—the writing of farewell notes.

"So what did you tell Mr. Petrie?" Kat asked when Jessie finished.

"Let's see," said Jessie. "I explained that I had to leave to attend to a family matter. I also thanked him for hiring me. And I said it was an experience of a lifetime to work for him."

She continued, "With any luck, the real translator they expected will be along shortly." Then she asked, "What did you write to Howard Carter?"

Kat smiled. "I also said thank you. For helping us catch the thieves. And for teaching me about archaeology."

Kat picked up her letter and read the end of it aloud.

> I hope you continue to keep digging. I know that some-day you will make a fantastic find. One that will catch the attention of the whole world.

"It certainly will," commented Jessie. "King Tut's tomb was one of the most important discoveries ever made in Egypt."

Kat sighed. "It would be exciting to see him uncover the tomb. I just don't want to wait around another 30 years!"

They folded the notes and left them on the cots. Someone was sure to spot them when they came in search of Jessie and Kat.

Now they set up the time machine. Taking off their medallions, they slipped them into place. At once the machine started to hum.

"We're ready," said Jessie. "Get your stuff, Kat." She hung the strap of the traveling bag over one arm. Kat put on her knapsack. Grabbing hold of the time machine, they carried it to the sunny doorway.

When the sunlight hit the medallions, the machine began to hum. Once again Kat and Jessie were swallowed up in a rush of wind and misty clouds.

The next thing they heard was the sound of excited barking. It was Newton!

Kat gazed around happily. They were home—back in the lab, back in their normal clothes.

She dropped to her knees. "Hey, Newton!" she cried, throwing her arms around the dog. "I'm glad to see you too!" She laughed as the dog joyfully licked her face.

"You'd think he hadn't seen you in days," Jessie commented. "When actually for Newton, it's just been a few seconds." She shook her head and gave the dog a friendly pat. "Why don't I unpack while you take him out for a walk?"

"Great idea," said Kat. "But first there's something I want to check out in my bedroom."

With Newton racing ahead of her, Kat dashed up the two

flights of stairs. At the door to her bedroom, she paused. There it stood, sitting in a pool of afternoon light: the bust of Nefertiti.

Kat studied the statue as though she'd never seen it before. The long neck, lovely face, and mysterious eyes of the Egyptian queen. She skimmed her fingers over the cool surface. "Hello again," she murmured.

"I never really thought about this before," Kat said to Newton. "But if it weren't for people like Petrie and Carter, we wouldn't know anything about her. We'd have no idea what she looked like or how she lived. The statue this is copied from—and all the pieces Carter found—would still be buried in the Egyptian desert."

Kat turned to go back downstairs. As she did, something flickered.

Strange, Kat thought. It was probably only a shadow. But for just a moment, it seemed that a smile had flitted across Nefertiti's face.

More to Explore

Have fun exploring more about everyday life and archaeological excavations in nineteenth-century Egypt. And there are great projects for you to do too!

The Story Behind the Story

The ruins of the ancient city of Amarna can still be visited today. Located close to the Nile River, Amarna was built in the fourteenth century B.C. by the pharaoh Akhenaten. Before Akhenaten, the Egyptians had worshiped many gods. But Akhenaten believed only one should be served: the sun god, Aten. The pharaoh built the city of Amarna to honor Aten.

After Akhenaten's death, the Egyptians returned to the worship of many gods. The temples and statues of Amarna were destroyed and the city deserted.

Thousands of years later, people interested in Egypt's past began to dig in Amarna. One of them was William Matthew Flinders Petrie. He was every bit as fussy and businesslike as Jessie reports. Before Petrie, some archaeologists actually used dynamite to uncover ancient treasures!

Petrie's methods were different. He insisted that everything be dug out carefully. He also wanted each fragment to be drawn and labeled to show where it had been located.

It's also a fact that Petrie hired a young man named Howard Carter. In 1892 Carter was only 18 years old. He had arrived in Egypt the year before to

96

work as an artist. His task was to copy the drawings found in ancient tombs.

A plaster cast was one of the many finds made at Amarna. And Petrie did ask Howard Carter's opinion about the object. The two men came to the conclusion that it was a cast that had been made from the face of the pharaoh after his death. This was accepted as fact for many years. However, a 1912 German excavation at Amarna uncovered many similar casts. We now know that these objects were only models used by sculptors when creating statues.

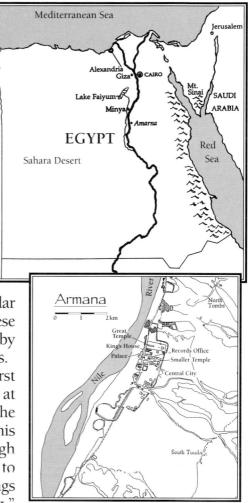

It's also true that Carter first tried his hand as an excavator at Amarna in 1892. And that he was worried about making his mark. He later wrote: "Although I had always had a longing to excavate…I had sad misgivings regarding this new undertaking."

Of course, Kat was not responsible for Carter's success at Amarna. His own hard work—and some luck—helped him make a significant find. Just as in the story, Carter explored an old rubbish heap near the ruins of the Great Temple. And there he discovered the remains of several statues of Akhenaten and his wife, Nefertiti. (However, the bust in Kat's bedroom, shown on pages 50 and 95, wasn't a copy of one of Carter's finds. That bust *was* found at Amarna. But it was unearthed by a group of German archaeologists years later, in 1922.)

Carter continued his work in Egypt for many years. In 1922 he made his greatest discovery of all—the tomb of Tutankhamen, the boy pharaoh.

Unlike many ancient tombs, King Tut's had never been robbed of its treasures. As the book shows, theft was a serious threat for archaeologists. Actually, this problem had existed for thousands of years. In fact, for some families, tomb robbing was a traditional way of making a living.

Tut's tomb turned out to be one of the most amazing finds in archaeology. Pictures of the glorious treasures Carter found there can be seen in books. And many of the actual objects are on display in museums around the world.

Nefertiti's Collar

Make a collar that even Queen Nefertiti would be proud to wear!

What you need

- 36"-wide felt (at least ½ yard)
- Fabric marker or pencil
- Measuring tape or yardstick
- Sewing scissors
- Large snap fastener
- Thread to match color of felt
- Sewing needle
- Materials for decorating the collar. See the suggestions at the end of the activity.

What you do

1. Measure and mark a 16" to 18" circle on the felt. Cut the circle, trying to make your curves smooth.

2. Measure and mark a 4" circle in the middle of the larger circle. Draw a straight line from the edge of the inside circle to the outer edge of the larger circle. Cut along the line as shown to make a slit in the back of the collar and a hole for your neck.

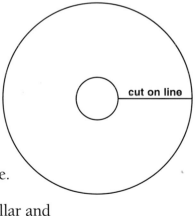

3. Sew one half of the snap fastener to the right side of the fabric, near the neckline edge of the slit. Sew the other

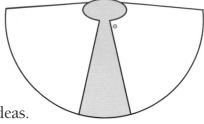

half to the wrong side of the fabric on the other side of the slit.

4. Decorate your Egyptian collar using any of the ideas below—or a combination of ideas.

Colorful additions

- Draw and cut out colorful paper "jewels." Use colored paper, fancy wrapping paper, aluminum foil, and other papers. Glue the jewels to your collar.

- Make a design with thin lines of glue. While the glue is wet, sprinkle glitter over it. Work on a small part of the collar at a time so the glue doesn't dry before you finish applying glitter. Be sure you use clear-drying glue.

- Sew shiny buttons or colorful beads to the collar.

- Make colorful patterns with sequins and then glue them in place. Be sure you use clear-drying glue.

- Collect leftover pieces of ribbon, braid, and other sewing trims. Arrange in a pattern, then glue or sew in place.

- Pin small safety pins all along the outside edge of the collar so they hang down like a jeweled fringe. You may want to add colorful beads to the pins.

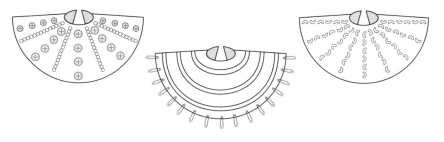

Egyptian Feast

Treat your family or friends to an Egyptian feast. Some food and decorating ideas can be found here. Ask an adult to help you with the cooking, or get permission to do it yourself.

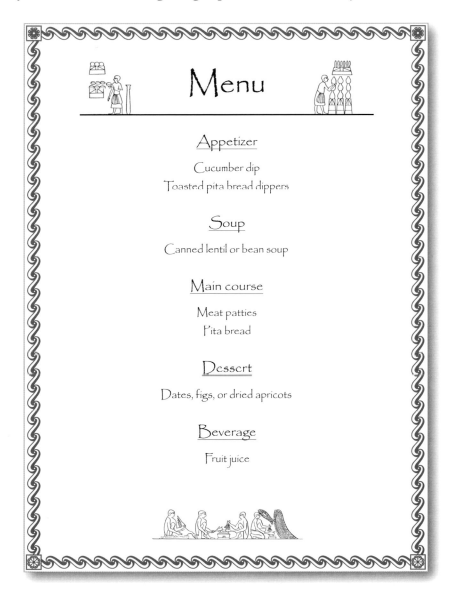

Menu

Appetizer

Cucumber dip
Toasted pita bread dippers

Soup

Canned lentil or bean soup

Main course

Meat patties
Pita bread

Dessert

Dates, figs, or dried apricots

Beverage

Fruit juice

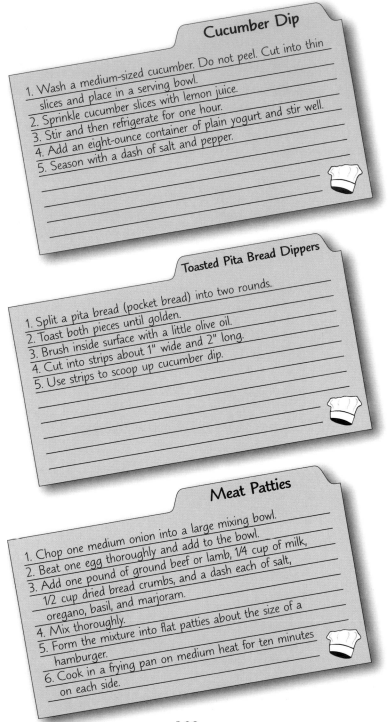

Cucumber Dip

1. Wash a medium-sized cucumber. Do not peel. Cut into thin slices and place in a serving bowl.
2. Sprinkle cucumber slices with lemon juice.
3. Stir and then refrigerate for one hour.
4. Add an eight-ounce container of plain yogurt and stir well.
5. Season with a dash of salt and pepper.

Toasted Pita Bread Dippers

1. Split a pita bread (pocket bread) into two rounds.
2. Toast both pieces until golden.
3. Brush inside surface with a little olive oil.
4. Cut into strips about 1" wide and 2" long.
5. Use strips to scoop up cucumber dip.

Meat Patties

1. Chop one medium onion into a large mixing bowl.
2. Beat one egg thoroughly and add to the bowl.
3. Add one pound of ground beef or lamb, 1/4 cup of milk, 1/2 cup dried bread crumbs, and a dash each of salt, oregano, basil, and marjoram.
4. Mix thoroughly.
5. Form the mixture into flat patties about the size of a hamburger.
6. Cook in a frying pan on medium heat for ten minutes on each side.

Dressy extras

- Create a place mat for each diner. You can make woven paper mats that look like they are made from palm branches. Or decorate paper mats with Egyptian hieroglyphics.

- Decorate the table with a bouquet of real or artificial flowers. The lotus is especially appropriate for an Egyptian-style feast.

- Place a small favor near each diner's plate. Mix together almonds, raisins, and dried apricots. Put a small amount of the mixture in the center of a piece of plastic wrap. Gather up the wrap and tie with a bit of ribbon.

Stardust Story Sampler

Stardust Classics books feature other heroines to believe in. Come explore with Laurel the Woodfairy and Alissa, Princess of Arcadia. Here are short selections from their books.

Selection from

LAUREL RESCUES THE PIXIES

Laurel fluttered along the path, with her friend Ivy close behind.

"Oh, Laurel," Ivy gasped. "You're not really going to go and stay with the pixies, are you?"

"Yes, I am," said Laurel. "The Eldest thinks it's a good idea. And so do I."

"Well, I don't," said Ivy. "I'm sure the Eldest would understand if you changed your mind."

By now they could hear the roar of Thunder Falls. Soon the falls and pond came into sight. Laurel flitted to a huge oak tree that grew near the waterfall. Her sunlit treehouse was nestled in the branches high above.

Laurel ignored the ladder and flew up to the porch. Ivy followed, still trying to think of a way to get her friend to stay.

Once inside, Laurel gazed around a bit sadly. She really couldn't imagine leaving her lovely home forever.

Still, she'd made up her mind to go. So that was exactly what she was going to do!

With a sigh, Laurel gathered up her traveling bag and began packing. She threw in some clean dresses and extra pairs of slippers.

"You're certainly packing a lot of things," noted Ivy. She'd been pacing the floor in silence while Laurel got ready.

"I may be gone a long time," replied Laurel.

"Oh, Laurel," moaned Ivy. "I'm afraid I'll never see you again."

"Don't worry," said Laurel, giving her friend a hug. "I'll be back. Even if I decide to stay with the pixies forever, I'll come to visit you."

"Stay forever?" exclaimed Ivy. "Please, Laurel! Don't even think that way! This is just supposed to be a visit."

"A visit!" echoed a familiar voice. "Why, you must be talking about me."

Laurel and Ivy whirled around. Outside on the porch stood Foxglove, a wide smile on his face.

The pixie smoothed down his shaggy black hair and straightened his fishskin tunic. "Sorry. I didn't mean to listen in like that," he said. "But it's hot out in the forest today. I was in a hurry to get up here where there's a breeze. So I came scrambling up the ladder without even a hello."

Laurel waved him inside. "You're always welcome. You know that."

As Foxglove stepped forward, his bright eyes lit on Laurel's traveling bag. "You're all ready for an adventure," he remarked. "I didn't know we had one planned!"

"I'm going away for a while," said Laurel.

Foxglove studied her face, noting that she seemed more sad than excited. "Going away?" he echoed. He glanced at Ivy, who only shook her head.

The pixie turned back to Laurel. "Would you like some company?" he asked with a smile.

"Well, actually, I'd *be* the company," Laurel said. "I

thought I'd come to stay with the pixies for a while. In your village."

Foxglove's smile suddenly disappeared.

Laurel felt her heart sink. Foxglove certainly didn't act happy about taking her home with him. Maybe he didn't want her around either.

Maybe she wasn't welcome anywhere!

Selection from

ALISSA AND THE DUNGEONS OF GRIMROCK

Princess Alissa sighed. "I wish I knew where Balin went and what he's doing now. I miss him. I even miss crabby old Bartok."

Lia laughed. The wizard's parrot had a habit of squawking "Begone!" at visitors—especially Alissa.

"What's really bothering me is that Balin has been gone so long," Alissa said. "I keep checking the tower. Yet there's no sign of him."

"I know," agreed Lia. "And it's strange that he's made two trips in the past month. I thought he almost never left the kingdom."

Alissa's eyes narrowed. "I'm worried," she admitted.

She reached up to touch the locket at her neck. Deep in thought, she ran her fingers over the crescent moon on its surface. More than two weeks ago, Balin had placed the locket around her neck. He'd told her not to take it off until he said so. His face, half-hidden by his flowing white beard, had been wrinkled with concern. She'd begged to know where he was going and why. But Balin had refused to tell her.

"He told me he'd be back in a week," continued Alissa. "Balin never breaks a promise. I know he's in trouble."

"What did he tell you about his first trip?" asked Lia.

"He said an old friend had sent for him," answered the princess. "Someone who needed his help. But when Balin arrived at the meeting place, no one was there. He had no idea who had tricked him. Or why."

"That *is* strange," commented Lia. "Still, don't you think Balin can take care of himself? You've seen how powerful his magic is."

"Remember, he says magic can't do everything," replied Alissa. "Besides, there's something else."

"What?"

"A wooden box is missing from the tower," Alissa revealed. "I noticed right after Balin left for the second time. He kept this strange box on a shelf. There was a dragon carved on its lid."

"Maybe Balin took the box with him," Lia suggested. "Do you know what he keeps in it?"

"No. And I asked him about it more than once. All he'd ever tell me was that the box must never leave Arcadia. So why would he take it with him?"

Lia shrugged. "I don't understand either. Though if he did, I'm sure he had a good reason." With that, she got to her feet. "It's time we got back to the castle."

Alissa rose and began helping Lia pack up their picnic basket.

Just as they finished packing, they heard a loud rustling

of leaves overhead. Both girls jumped when something tumbled to their feet, screeching horribly.

Alissa recognized their visitor. "It's Bartok!" she said to Lia. "Balin must have returned!"

The girls looked around for Balin. There was no sign of the wizard.

Alissa bent closer to check on Bartok. The bird flapped his wings furiously. His feathers were dirty and mussed. And his eyes were wild—even wilder than usual.

She picked up the parrot. "Settle down," she ordered. "Now tell me, where is Balin?"

Bartok glared at her. Loudly he squawked a single word: "Captured!"

"Lia!" cried Alissa in a low voice. "He has to mean Balin! Balin must have been captured!"

STARDUST CLASSICS titles are written under pseudonyms. Authors work closely with Margaret Hall, executive editor of Just Pretend.

Ms. Hall has devoted her professional career to working with and for children. She has a B.S. and an M.S. in education from the State University of New York at Geneseo. For many years, she taught as a classroom and remedial reading teacher for students from preschool through upper elementary. Ms. Hall has also served as an editor with an educational publisher and as a consultant for the Iowa State Department of Education. She has a long history as a freelance writer for the school market, authoring several children's books as well as numerous teacher resources.

KAZUHIKO SANO was born in Tokyo, Japan. He came to the United States to study at the Academy of Art College in San Francisco. After graduation he stayed in the United States and worked as a freelance illustrator. At the same time, he continued his art education, eventually earning a Master of Fine Arts degree.

Mr. Sano works full-time as an illustrator. His art was featured on a movie poster for *The Return of the Jedi* and on promotional materials for the Star Wars trilogy. He has also done paintings of dinosaurs for *Scientific American* magazine and designed a series of United States postal stamps.

Kazuhiko Sano is married and has two young children. He and his family live in Mill Valley, California.